Hoochie Coochie

G. W. Reynolds III

This is a work of fiction. While, as in all fiction, the literary perceptions and insights are based on experience, all names, characters, places, and incidents are either products of the author's imagination or are used fictitiously. No reference to any real person is intended or inferred.

ISBN: 0-9777290-3-6

Published and distributed by:
High-Pitched Hum Publishing
321 15th Street North
Jacksonville Beach, FL 32250

www.highpitchedhum.net

Contact G.W. Reynolds III at www.jettyman.com

Hoochie Coochie

G. W. Reynolds III

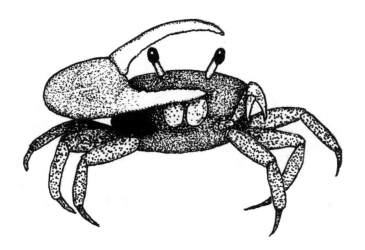

PRELUDE

Mary C. stood in front of Mr. John King's haunted house next to her new red Chevrolet Corvette. Jason was standing with her holding his son Billy in his arms. Mary C. was talking, and as usual Jason was listening.

"I'm gonna find that girl if it's the last thing I do. I knew she had the necklace, and she was gonna run. I knew it all the time and I didn't go with my gut. That won't happen again." She reached out her hands and took Billy from Jason's arms. "Go tell Fabian I need to see him. I want that girl and that necklace. If the necklace is gone, I still want that girl."

Rebecca Milkduds Coolie drove her truck up to a wooden gate that crossed the dirt road in front of her. There was a sign on the gate that read: *If we don't know you, don't take this road.* She had no desire to make the ride to her Aunt Annie's house and fortress located about two miles down that muddy road. Rebecca had considered her few options and came to the conclusion it would be the best place to hide until she could develop a plan of action to leave the area and take Miss Stark's antique necklace with her. She knew her Aunt Annie would not suspect anything after she heard about the deaths of her father and brothers. Surely, Aunt Annie would take her in and protect her after such a tragic and traumatic ordeal. After all, Rebecca's father was Annie's brother.

Annie was more of a man than a woman. Rebecca knew she would most likely have to deal with her aunt's aggressive nature and the strange men and women who were living with her. She was ready for whatever came her way, and she did need a place to stay.

Throughout the years, Aunt Annie's home had evolved into a true den of thieves, cutthroats, murderers, pimps, whores, gamblers, and men and women of extremely low moral fiber. You could get almost anything you wanted on Aunt Annie's island. Nothing was cheap, but nothing was off limits for the right price. It was a true barter town. Sex and perversion were the number one sellers with drugs and guns a close second. One of the small houses about two hundred yards away from the main house was mostly for dice and poker games. They called it the Shed. You could bargain to have something stolen or someone maimed or even killed. You could get it all on Black Hammock Island.

Between fifty and sixty individuals lived on the island with Aunt Annie year round. They were her extended family. She called her island family, and workers her "fiddler crabs." Some left from time to time, but usually returned after completing their work off and away from the island. An average of a hundred people passed through each week looking for sexual pleasures, a place to sleep the night and hide out, or to sell ill gotten gains. Most visitors were gone before nightfall unless there was a special event or party going on.

The locals and regular customers came for sex and drugs and to roll the dice or sit at the poker tables, but once in a while an abused wife would bring her money and body to barter to have her slime ball husband "drawn and quartered."

Everyone paid Aunt Annie her fair share. She had amassed a huge fortune in money and goods as she was given a portion of each evil deal that transpired on the island. No one cheated her, or failed to pay his or her tribute. Every low life honored her with a monetary gift after each deal was completed. It was the way it was. The island protected them and gave them a sanctuary to do their unholy business. Aunt Annie was the Queen and the King of the human muck and mud of the Earth. Her fiddler crabs lived in the mud with her.

There was a spot about fifty yards behind the main house where the water from the St. Johns River found its way into a little cove. It was Aunt Annie's favorite place on the entire island. When the tide was low it was full of the big claw fiddler crabs and their female companions. She liked watching the crabs run sideways in and out of their holes in the mud. Aunt Annie would have one of the young people living on the island catch the quick moving mini-crabs so she could use them for bait when she went fishing. Aunt Annie loved to fish, and her island was the perfect place. She even rented boats and had her own bait and tackle shop on the grounds. The cove was also a well hidden waterway for drug and gun runners to float up and sell their goods to one of Aunt Annie's fiddler crabs. Aunt Annie's fondness for the real fiddler crabs inspired her to call her loyal workers by the same name. She was never around when the drug or other deals were made.

Even on the island of sin and degradation, Aunt Annie did have one rule: no child molesters. She had spent her early childhood years being raped and sodomized by an uncle who had taken her to raise after her mother and father died. Aunt Annie had also been a member of the Florida female chain gang and suffered through two horrible years of sexual abuse at the hands of the male guards. She hated men with a passion but would tolerate them as long as they had money in their pockets. If you didn't have and spend money, you didn't stay on the island very long.

The main house looked similar to John King's haunted house. There was no doubt it was built during the same era of architecture. The house slept twenty comfortably with six upstairs bedrooms and an attic. All the bedrooms were used during the day for sex business and sometimes drug business, if the person wanted to buy, use and stay.

Aunt Annie had become an expert at recognizing the true intruders to the island. For years she had used armed guards at the gate and on the road leading to the island. But now the warning signs seemed to be enough to scare the unwanted away. Only the ones who knew Aunt Annie, or had done business on the island, came calling.

Once in a while someone on the run would show up looking for a safe haven. Aunt Annie would talk to them to decide if they were

who they said they were. They could either stay or move on; it was
her call. Some never left the island. They became fiddler crabs or
were buried there. Some of the women were working off debts they
owed to Aunt Annie. After their debts were paid in full, they were
allowed to leave, but most came back when they needed help or
more money. For some of the women, degrading themselves to
survive had become a vicious cycle.

Rebecca opened the truck door and stepped out onto the muddy
ground. She pushed the gate open, and got back into the truck.
After a deep breath, she felt her heart pound when she pressed the
gas pedal down with her muddy bare foot and headed toward Black
Hammock Island.

CHAPTER ONE

Fabian Moore was sitting on his front porch with his sister Theda. She held her baby in her arms and was rocking him in a wicker chair. The funerals were over, and the relatives had all gone. Fabian and Theda had lost their father, Stoddard Moore, a close childhood friend, Eli Sallas, and another friend, Joe Croom. Fabian had a hand in the revenge killing of Earnest Coolie, and his two sons, Duck and Bucket. It had been seven days of death, and pure evil. It was a typical week in Mayport, Florida, U.S.A.

Fabian and Theda both looked up when they heard Jason's truck coming into the front yard. The truck stopped near the porch steps. Jason stepped out of the truck and walked toward his two friends. Fabian nodded. "Come on up and sit with us."

Jason stepped up onto the porch. "Mama wants to see ya, if that's okay."

Fabian smiled. "I'll always come when she wants me." He stood up and turned to Theda. "You gonna be alright here for a little while?"

Theda looked down and hesitated with her answer. Fabian looked back at Jason. "She's still a little skittish." He looked at Theda again. "How 'bout Jason stayin' so I can see what Mary C. wants?" Theda nodded, but did not lift her head. Fabian faced Jason again. "Can ya stay? I'll be back as soon as I can." Jason nodded, but like Theda, he had no words.

Rebecca looked out the driver's side window to read the second sign on the dirt road. *Beware of the bad dogs and the bad fiddler crabs.* Her heart raced again in her chest behind her huge breasts. A group of turkey buzzards eating a dead armadillo drew her attention away from the sign. The nasty black birds hopped away from the carcass as the truck went by, but they did not fly. They waited for the truck to pass then hopped back to their meal.

The next sign gave this warning: *It's still not too late to go back.* Rebecca knew she was only a short distance from the main entrance to the island. Cars and trucks were parked on both sides of the road in front of her. She heard voices and cheering as the truck moved slowly down the road. Something big was going on at Aunt Annie's. There was a last sign: *It's too late now.*

Rebecca drove past a large, noisy crowd of men and women. They had formed a human circle around a chicken wire fence. She knew from her past experience that the loud cheering crowd was watching two mutant roosters in a cock fight. To the left side of the road, she saw at least twenty dogs tied to separate wooden posts. Each dog was tied to a short leash line so they could not reach another. The wild creatures barked, growled and pulled at the chains holding them from attacking man or beast near them. Again, Rebecca knew from her past the dogs were there to fight and possibly kill each other for the amusement of the spectators. She knew it was Fight Week on Black Hammock Island.

Theda lowered her sleeping baby down in his crib. Jason sat on the couch in the living room. She had always known she would give herself to Jason if the opportunity ever presented itself. It was the perfect time and place. Her mature nature gave her the courage to make her fantasy come true. She took off her clothes, and put on a blue bathrobe over her naked body. Jason looked up when she entered the living room. The blue terrycloth robe was open in the front exposing her young naked body. She was small and reminded him of seeing his mother in her white terrycloth bath robe, and how she usually wore it when men were visiting.

BEWARE OF THE BAD DOGS AND THE BAD FIDDLER CRABS!

CROBERTSON
5' 2006

Jason knew Theda was there for the taking, and he had never refused such an offer in his young life. He stood up and pulled down on the robe causing it to drop off of her shoulders and fall down to her feet. She stood there completely naked. Even though she just had a baby, Theda's body was young and still firm. She was a petite young woman with a little softness visible on her lower stomach. Her legs and buttocks were firm and in perfect proportion with the rest of her body. Her milk-filled breasts added to her pleasing appearance.

"I've seen the way you look at me. I've wanted to be with you ever since I was a little girl. I don't know why, but I knew we would be alone like this one day. I hope you feel the same."

Jason could not recall looking at Theda in a certain way to make her think he wanted her, but if she felt that he did, so be it. He did not respond. Theda had more to share.

"If you're worried about me tellin' Fabian, that will never happen. If you don't tell him, he'll never know. But, we should hurry just in case he comes back sooner than we thought."

Jason's animal blood ran like wildfire through his veins, and settled between his legs in a matter of seconds. His manliness pushed against the front of his pants. Theda reached out, unbuckled his belt and unzipped his pants. He helped her push them down to the floor. He stepped out of the pants and stood there bottomless, but still wearing his shirt. Theda reached down and held him in her hand. The heat and hardness took her breath away. She had been with a few young boys, and one nasty man like Duck Coolie, but she had never had a man like Jason. She was worried about the size of his manliness. She thought she would not be able to handle what Jason had to offer.

"I might still be a little sore down there, but I don't care." Theda had no idea Jason didn't care either.

Rebecca stopped while a group of men walked past the front of the truck. No one seemed to pay any attention to the beauty behind the wheel. After they passed, she drove up to the front of the house and stopped at the porch steps. She looked through the dirty front windshield and recognized her Aunt Annie sitting in a chair on the porch. Two women sat with Annie, one at each side. Rebecca's heart raced again, and her throat went dry when she realized the last sign was right. "It was too late now."

Jason sat on the couch and Theda sat across him. She was wet with desire, and her worries were eased when his manliness slid deep into her with one push. She moaned from the instant depth of the penetration, but the feeling of pleasure far outweighed any discomfort she was experiencing. Jason liked the heat at first, but he did not pound Theda as he would Margie. He was gentle and concerned with her post-birth condition. When he pushed deep inside her, she began to move her hips and moan with pleasure. At first Jason allowed her to push when she wanted. Theda showed no signs of pain or discomfort as their pumping motion intensified. Each time she pressed down with her hips, Jason pushed up with his own pelvic thrust.

Theda's noises and movement told Jason she was willing and able to do what ever he wanted. He pushed her petite body up, breaking their sexual connection. His sudden exit surprised Theda for a second, but when she realized he was only repositioning her, she moved with him as if they were old dance partners, and she was following his lead. Jason turned her around, and she was on her knees facing the couch. She felt moisture running down the inside of her legs, but again she didn't care; nothing mattered at that moment. There are times when nothing else matters.

Jason knelt down behind her. What felt like an electric shock jolted Theda's young and tender body when Jason entered her from behind. With his first thrust, he was as deep as he could possibly go. Theda tried not to scream, but that was impossible. The combination of pain and pleasure was just too much for her young mind and body. Her screams were like a wild banshee. Jason felt he had damaged her in some way, so he hesitated to make another sexual thrust. The echo of her scream lingered for a second or two. Jason waited as Theda took a deep breath.

"Don't stop, please, but do it one push at a time." She did not think she could survive a repeated pounding.

Jason pushed again. She screamed again; another push, another scream. Jason smiled as he gave her two quick thrusts in a row. Her scream turned blood curdling. Jason smiled again and started · pumping in and out in rapid succession with no regard for Theda's condition or screams. No one had ever reacted to Jason like she did. He loved every second of it.

Miss Margaret sat on her front porch in one of her wooden rocking chairs. Her eldest daughter, Margie, pushed open the screen door, and stepped out onto the porch. Her youngest, Sofia, followed her older sister.

"Good morning, you two."

The two girls answered in unison stereo. "Good morning, Mother."

Miss Margaret had two boxes at her feet and held a book in her hand. Sofia saw the boxes first. "What's in the boxes?"

Miss Margaret held up a thin book. "I was just looking through these old children's books I used to read to y'all when you were little girls. There's a lot of memories in these boxes." She handed Sofia the book she was holding.

Sofia's beautiful face and ice-blue eyes lit up. "Oh Mother, this was my favorite!" Sofia opened the book and began turning the pages. Margie looked at the book and rolled her eyes. She knew Sofia actually considered herself a "Sleeping Beauty." She always had.

"There is no Prince Charming to ride in and wake you up, Sofia. Not the way you snore." Sofia cut her eyes at Margie. Margie did not care. "Got to get to the store. It's clean-the-shelves day, and it's our turn."

Miss Margaret knew sarcasm when she heard it, but she would not respond to Margie's little dig. She changed the subject. "I'm giving these old books to the church to sell at the annual bazaar next week. They're in such good shape, and we have no use for them now."

Sofia's heart was still soft, even if she thought she had changed after killing a man. "I don't know, Mother. It's like giving away our memories."

Margie had to roll her eyes again. "None of us are little girls anymore; let someone else enjoy the books. The dust on 'em should tell us it's time to give them away. Let's go. Susan will think we've forgotten her, and I don't want to listen to her mouth if we're late."

Sofia kissed her mother on the cheek. "I love you, Mother." She followed Margie to the family station wagon.

Fabian sat on Mr. John King's front porch with Mary C. They had already exchanged hugs, kisses and pleasantries. Mary C. was always straight to the point. "Where ya think that girl's gone to?"

It was no surprise to Fabian when he heard the question. "I'm not sure, but we might have a lead."

Mary C.'s eyes were ablaze. "I didn't follow my gut this time. It's my fault. I want her and the necklace. I think I want her even worse than I want the necklace. She looked deep into my eyes and she snaked me, dammit. She snaked me."

Fabian could see that Mary C. was on the edge. He had always been smart, and he knew when to be quiet. He would listen and do whatever Mary C. wanted.

Theda's screams filled the house. The noise bounced off the ceiling and walls. They were both in a sexual trance. Nothing else mattered for either one of them. Jason would not stop, and she had no power or desire to stop him. Jason moaned and added to the noise as he released his sexual fluids deep inside Theda's body. The heat inside Theda was overwhelming, and she had never felt anything like it before. Her body went limp as Jason moved away from her and she fell onto the couch. Jason lay with his back on the floor. He stared up at the ceiling. He thought he could still hear the echoes of Theda's screams, but he realized it was Theda's baby crying. Theda came out of her sexual stupor and heard the baby, too. She stood up from the couch and stepped over Jason's body. Jason looked up and saw blood running down the inside of her legs.

Aunt Annie was a big woman. Not fat, big. She stood six feet, three inches, weighed two hundred-twenty pounds, and if there was such a thing as being "big boned," Aunt Annie fit the condition. She stood up from her seat when she realized her niece, Rebecca Coolie, had come for a visit.

Aunt Annie wore long camouflaged army pants, tucked into calf-high, black, lace-up army issue boots. Her stained, white, v-neck t-shirt had little success in covering her two huge sagging breasts and her big Dixie-cup nipples. The wobbling motion of her braless breasts brought instant attention to the movement under the thin white shirt. Folks just had to look. Her hair was cropped off short and parted on the left side with an Elvis pompadour in the front.

The woman sitting to Aunt Annie's left was gorgeous. Rebecca looked past Aunt Annie and the woman stared back. She had long blonde hair and deep blue eyes. Her slender body was tight and muscular. She wore short cut-off dungarees that only covered her buttocks and pelvic area. A bra-like bathing suit top covered her ample breasts.

The other woman was a gross contrast to the beautiful blonde. At first she looked to Rebecca more like a man than Aunt Annie. She had a short crew-cut hair style, butch wax and all. Then Rebecca looked closer. Crew Cut had a pretty face, and her body

was that of a woman. Her face and body were both a contradiction
to the appearance she wanted. Her face was soft; she wore lip-stick
and make-up. Her body was athletic and she looked hard as a rock.
In a strange way she was actually attractive even with the crew-cut.
The two women remained seated as Aunt Annie met Rebecca at the
steps. "Look at you, girl."

Rebecca gave a half-smile as Aunt Annie hugged her and held
her close.   Rebecca's hard breasts were crushed against Aunt
Annie's huge sagging breasts causing at least a full foot of flesh to
separate the rest of their bodies. Aunt Annie smelled of body odor,
snuff tobacco and what Rebecca thought was a Slim-Jim sausage.
She was a triple threat. Aunt Annie ended the hug and held Rebecca
at arms' length.

"What a woman you turned out to be. I never expected to see
you out this way again. I figured y'all forgot about your old Aunt
Annie. Ya by yaself?"

Rebecca looked around at all the people and hesitated to answer.
Aunt Annie was excited. "Hell, girl, it's Fight Week on the island."

Rebecca nodded. "I thought so. I remember Pa talkin' bout it."

"We fight dogs and roosters all week, and then the main event on
Saturday is man-to-man, the best of the best. The baddest two men
walkin' this Earth will be here to settle it all. I get chills just
thinkin' bout it."

Rebecca had allowed her aunt to take over the conversation.
"Settle what?"

Aunt Annie looked back at the two women on the porch then
looked back at Rebecca. "Hell girl, we got Jack Jackal Jarvis comin'
to my island. Sometimes they call him triple "J" and a few other
choice names. Jackal's from some fishin' town in Maryland. He's
been makin' a big name for his self in the South by knockin' other
men into the next week. He's gonna match his skills against a
monster of a man out of Palm Valley.   His given name is Virgil
Hartley, but he goes by Grave Digger. Ain't that a great fighin'
name? Grave Digger. I love it. They'll meet here Saturday at high
noon and settle the question of who's the baddest man on the planet.
I can't talk about it no more. I'm gettin' too excited. I'll cum in my
pants."   Aunt Annie's quick change of subject and tone of voice

surprised Rebecca. "Why ya out here alone like this, girl? Where's ya daddy?"

Rebecca found the courage to answer. "Somethin' awful happened, and I had no place to go." Rebecca wasn't sure if the look on Aunt Annie's face was one of concern or disgust. She was hard to read.

"What happened, girl?"

Rebecca's big breasts rose and fell as she took a deep breath. "Pa's dead. The boys, too."

Aunt Annie's facial expression or lack of did not change. "All three of 'em?"

"Yes, ma'am. Pa killed a man in Mayport and then his son come and killed Pa and the boys. He was one of them army fighters with them green hats."

Aunt Annie looked back at the two women. "Green Beret, huh?"

Crew Cut nodded. "Most likely."

Aunt Annie turned back to Rebecca. "This one man killed Duck and Bucket, too?" She bit her bottom lip and asked Rebecca to clarify what she said. "So you're tellin' that one man killed all three of 'em?" Rebecca nodded her head. "Sounds like a bad man."

"Yes, ma'am. His sister had Duck's baby. They took her and the baby. The boys had their way with the girl and Duck was gonna keep her and his son."

Aunt Annie shook her head. "So, this bad man went to your house and took her and the baby back?"

"Yes, ma'am."

Aunt Annie turned and looked at the two women again, but she talked to Rebecca. "Jesus girl, that's a crazy story. Why the hell would Earnest steal a baby? He probably had cause to kill the man, but stealin' a baby just don't fit."

"Pa didn't want the baby at first. Later, Pa changed his mind 'cause he thought it would be even more revenge against Stoddard Moore if Pa kept his grandson. It really got crazy. When we was leavin' the Moore house a big mean dog attacked Pa and tore him up bad. After the man with that green hat killed 'em all, I got scared, so here I am."

"You mixed up in all this, girl?"

"I guess bein' part of the family puts me right in the middle. And the fact I helped Pa get into the house so he could kill the man."

"Po-leese after you?"

"They told me not to leave, but here I am."

Rebecca stepped up onto the front porch as Aunt Annie put her arm around her shoulder. She turned toward the two women. "This here's my niece, Becky. Ain't she beautiful?" Both women nodded, but did not smile or respond. Rebecca wore her own version of the cut-off dungaree shorts.

Theda walked back into the living room. Jason had dressed and was sitting back on the couch. She was also dressed. He could tell she had cleaned herself. She sat down next to him. "Little Sammy fell back to sleep. I must'a woke him up with all the noise I was makin'. I'm so embarrassed. You must think I'm a child."

Jason had no such thought in his mind. "You alright?"

She put her head down. "It was just a little messy, but I'm really fine. I'm more than fine. It was wonderful." She bowed her head again. "Now, I'm really embarrassed."

Jason smiled. "Don't be. You have no reason to be embarrassed. You're right. It was wonderful."

Mr. John King walked out onto his front porch. "Mary C., you seen…oh, hey, Fabian I didn't mean to interrupt y'all. I thought you was out here alone. Didn't know you had company."

Mary C. nodded. "What is it, John? We just talkin' bout how to find that girl and get the necklace back."

"I think that's worth talkin' bout. But, I was wonderin' if you had seen that white doily that sits on the arm of the chair in the living room? I've looked everywhere and it's just gone."

Mary C. couldn't resist. "Maybe your new friend, Norman, had to use it to wipe his skinny dead ass." Mary C. was good for a surprising rude and crude comment from time to time.

"Now, Mary C. that's an awful picture to put in my mind this early in the day. What ya want to say that for? If I do find it now, I don't think I could put it back on the chair. Maybe it was a ghost that took it, but I don't think they need to wipe their butts anymore."

"I don't know about that, John. That can't be you flushing the toilet at night all the time."

Mr. King shook his head and knew when he was beaten. Fabian had to smile at Mr. King's sarcasm and Mary C.'s wit. They both had a dry and strange sense of humor. Neither one knew how close Mary C.'s thought came to what had actually happened to the white doily. It was Margie who used the doily to wipe her ass. She had taken it with her when she left, hoping to wash it clean and return it at another time.

Fabian looked over toward Miss Margaret's store as Margie and Sofia got out of the green family station wagon. They walked into the store. Mary C. saw them, too. She looked at Fabian.

"Can't you young bucks get enough of them girls? How many you had since ya got back?"

Again, Fabian was not surprised by Mary C.'s question. He would always tell her his mind. He knew she liked it that way. He did, too. "I like Margie. The others are just children. Sofia's the prettiest but still a child. I like Margie."

Mary C. had more. "And the Coolie girl?"

Fabian wanted to lie, but he knew he couldn't. "She's the most incredible thing I've ever seen. I'm sorry she left. As you say, 'she snaked me,' too."

"But, you'd take her back tomorrow wouldn't ya?"

"Today, if she was here."

Rebecca Coolie finished telling her story to Aunt Annie. She left out the part where she helped Theda and the baby escape from the evil clutches of her father and brothers. She didn't mention the fact she had stayed with Fabian and Theda Moore or that she had given herself to the man who killed her father and brothers. The topic of the multi-million dollar antique necklace was never brought up either. Women like Aunt Annie, however, knew things, and she knew her niece was only telling her part of the story.

Mr. King stood alone in his living room. He looked around and whispered so Mary C. and Fabian could not hear him. "Norman, if you took the doily or you know which ghost did, get it back for me. My Aunt Viola crocheted them just before she was killed. I'd really hate to lose one of 'em."

Aunt Annie walked ahead of Rebecca as they moved through the upstairs hallway. "I got a hell of a business here, girl. I was gonna retire this year and call it quits, but the money's bigger and easier than ever. I don't need to retire to some island. I got my own island right here."

Stella Croom sat on her dead son's bed and touched his pillow. Her eyes were dry, but full of hurt and hate--hate for Mary C. Her husband, Big Joe Croom, stood at the door. She looked up. "I want you out of this house today. You can't live here until that woman's dead. Either you do it or have it done. I don't care how, just do it. We don't speak or sleep together until her funeral is over and she's in the ground. Go sleep on the boat, go sleep in the woods, go sleep in hell. Go live up to your name, Big Joe." She stared a hole in his breaking heart and empty soul. He moved away from the door.

Rebecca could hear the sound of music coming from one of the rooms. She stopped to listen to the honky tonk beat of the music and read the sign over the door. She read it out loud. "Hoochie Coochie." She felt Aunt Annie's hot Slim Jim sausage breath on her neck from behind.

"That's the Hoochie Coochie room. Our motto is--*You got the Hoochie, we got the Coochie.* That's funny ain't it? I love sayin' 'Hoochie Coochie.' I like the way it rolls off the tongue. That's funny ain't it?" Rebecca did not have time to respond. "And ya know there's a dance called the Hoochie Coochie. You'd be surprised how many men and women want to see women dance the Hoochie Coochie. Hell, girl, we even have all night Hoochie Coochie parties with dancin' only and no sex 'til dawn. While you're here it might be a good thing for you to learn to dance the Hoochie Coochie. It just might come in handy down the road one day."

Aunt Annie left Rebecca in one of the bedrooms and went to see to her customers. Friday night was only a few hours away. The big main event would take place at high-noon on Saturday. Rebecca stayed in the room. She had no desire to walk among the dog and cock-fighting spectators. Rebecca was mentally and physically exhausted. She lay down on the bed and was going to rest her heavy eyes for a few minutes.

Theda stood at the front door with Jason. They were kissing passionately. The kiss ended and she whispered in his ear. "I wish we had more time. I'd like to do it again. I'll do better next time."

Jason would never understand Theda's feelings of low-self esteem. He thought she was remarkable and considered her one of best he had the pleasure of kneeling behind. He did not respond to her words but instead kissed her again. Theda knew how quiet Jason was, so it didn't matter if he talked or not. She had been in love with him since she started touching herself in the third grade. She slowly dropped to her knees onto the floor, unbuckled his belt and unzipped his pants again. She was excited beyond her limits as she wrapped her wet lips around his thick member.

Jason eased his body down and sat back in the chair behind him. He moved slowly so Theda would be able to keep her mouth in contact with him. Jason smiled when Theda's ability reminded him of Peggy's oral talents. He knew Theda had done that before. He pushed Theda's head down with his hand. It was his style. If he had a strawberry Nehi he would have taught Theda one of Peggy's tricks. On second thought, he didn't want to have to use Babo cleanser to get the red stain off of his manliness. Jason looked down at the back of Theda's bobbing head. He couldn't believe the fifteen year-old new mother who was sister to his best friend was eating him alive. He loved it. Jason was born for such pleasure. Theda let the baby cry.

Officer David Boos sat at his desk at the Atlantic Beach Police station. He held a black book in his hand. His partner, Paul Short, walked in and joined him at the desk.

"Is that it?"

Officer Boos nodded. "That's it. It was right there in his desk. You gotta see this thing. Our Mr. Butler was obsessed with the one and only Mary C., but what a collection of information. No wonder he was so crazy when it came to her and that strange boy of hers." He turned to one of the pages. "He's got names, dates, what he thought happened and what was actually told by Mary C. and an army of Mayport citizens."

Officer Paul Short was interested in the life, deaths and times of Mary C., but there was something else on his mind. "Don't get too caught up in that little book right yet. We need to put it up for now and talk about our visit to Black Hammock Island."

Rebecca woke up from a sex-filled dream and realized she was not alone in the bed. Blondie and Crew Cut were sucking on her breasts. She felt a warm moist sensation between her legs and she knew Aunt Annie and her long tongue was the third member of her attackers. Milkduds Coolie closed her eyes and allowed the triple team to continue. The threesome rotated positions so each one would have a turn at the different parts of Rebecca's incredible body. It felt good and she did need a place to hide.

Rebecca thought about Fabian Moore and that he would kill the three lesbians and then lean her over the couch and enter her from behind. She missed Fabian and Theda, but it was Mary C. she feared. Rebecca knew the evil one could see deep into her soul.

The three attackers moved from the bed to the floor. No hands or lips touched Rebecca. She opened her eyes to see Blondie on the floor with her legs spread wide open. Rebecca could see the back of Aunt Annie's head buried between the long white legs. The woman smiled at Rebecca as Aunt Annie grunted, snorted and made pig-like noises. Crew Cut straddled Blondie's head with her naked body and moved her crotch against her face. Rebecca's heart jumped, and she felt a sharp pain when she saw three men sitting in chairs in the dark corners of the room. They were watching the women's oral performance. You could watch sex being performed for five dollars. You could participate in an orgy for ten dollars and you could have one-on-one sex with the individual of your choice for twenty dollars, all money paid in advance to Aunt Annie.

When Aunt Annie saw her niece Rebecca Milkduds Coolie step out of the truck, all she saw at first were dollar signs. Rebecca could not see the faces of the men in the room, but they were there, alright.

Officer Boos and Officer Short sat at the desk looking down at a map of the St. Johns River and the surrounding area. Officer Boos made an observation. "There's only one road in and the same road out. Can you believe we got permission to take a look at what's goin' on out there? I hope we can pull off our little masquerade and we don't get ourselves killed. Everyone says it's a dangerous place, especially for the law."

Officer Short was excited about the possibilities. "This is a career-changing opportunity. I wonder why nobody's tried to find out about that place."

"I think they did years ago, but when sex, drugs, gamblin' and big easy money are involved, police corruption's not far away. I wouldn't be surprised if that place was protected right now by some high public official collecting his share of the booty every month."

Officer Boos nodded in agreement. "Let's hope we don't run into anyone we know out there, but it's likely we will." Both police officers had no idea they were going to be active members and participants in the biggest and most outrageous coincidence since the beginning of time.

The eldest of the three men sitting in the room stood up and walked past the three women on the floor. Rebecca's heart raced when she looked up at him as he came and stood at the side of the bed. He glared down at her incredible body. Her breasts pointed at him as if they beckoned his mouth. He had never seen a woman like Rebecca Milkduds Coolie.

He wasn't a handsome man, but he wasn't ugly either. His hair was grey and his face was lined from the weather and hard work. He smelled of Old Spice, making him a cut above most of the men on Black Hammock Island. The room was silent as he stood there. He did not take his eyes off of Rebecca's body, but he talked to Aunt Annie. His voice had a haunting crack to it. "How much? Just me!"

Aunt Annie did not hesitate with her evil answer. "One hour, one hundred dollars, cash money."

Rebecca's heart pounded in her chest. She saw the man's lip quiver as he took a deep breath. "Done! Now, get out, all of ya!"

The twins, Chuck and Buck Croom, sat on a big wooden spool in their yard. Their brother Pee Wee was drinking from the water hose. Pee Wee was older, but much smaller and weaker than the twins. If humans gave birth to runts, Pee Wee qualified for the title. The three boys watched their father Big Joe Croom throw a bag of clothes into his truck and get into the front cab. They knew he was angry. They had heard the fights between their parents since their brother's funeral was over. Pee Wee's eyes filled with tears as the truck drove away. The twins had no tears. They were far too mean.

The room was quiet and empty except for Rebecca and the older man. She was still lying in the bed on her back with her frontal attributes causing a raging fire in the man's loins. Even with a life-time of sexual experiences and activity with lovers, one night stands and whores, he had never been with a woman like Milkduds Coolie.

His raspy voice cracked and sent a shivering chill down Rebecca's flawless spine as he sat down next to her on the edge of the bed.

"The name's Thurber, Julius Thurber. I had to take on another name when I came here, so folks call me Quasimodo around here, but you're gonna call me Daddy. You understand?"

Rebecca Coolie was no fool. She had the same survival traits possessed by Mary C. "Yes, Daddy, I do."

Julius grinned a big tobacco stained smile after her perfect response. "You got a name?"

"Yes, Daddy. Rebecca. Rebecca Coolie."

"I'm gonna call ya Esmeralda."

Even though it was a strange request, Rebecca did not hesitate with the correct answer. "Yes, Daddy, of course. You can call me whatever you want."

"Esmeralda will do just fine. You know the story about the beautiful Gypsy girl and the bell ringer?"

"No Daddy, I don't think so."

"I'll tell you that story when I have more time, but we've talked long enough, don't ya think so?" He didn't care if she answered. He took off his clothes and crawled into the bed.

Julius Thurber reached out with one of his big callus hands and squeezed one of her hard oversized breasts. His hand shook at the firmness and size of the flesh he held. Rebecca's body quivered again when he reached out with his other hand and touched her other breast. He was missing the thumb and the index finger on that hand. It felt strange when only the three remaining digits squeezed her tightly. He saw her look at his hand and felt her uneasy body quake.

"Had to have part of my hand cut off 'cause it was infected. It was that or die. Don't be scared. It's just ugly, it won't hurt ya."

Theda started choking and pulled her head away when Jason exploded and released his hot sexual fluids deep down her throat. She tried to complete the act and take all Jason could give, but not this time. Once again she felt inadequate and ashamed, but that was just her foolish thinking and a moment of immaturity. Jason thought she was outrageously gifted.

Fabian told Mary C. all he knew about Rebecca Coolie. He also said he thought maybe Theda might know more about where she had gone. Mary C. appreciated his honesty, but she expected no less from him.

Julius "Quasimodo" Thurber didn't treat Rebecca Milkduds Coolie like one of the whores he had encountered. He knew she was the most beautiful woman he had ever been with or would ever be with again. He actually considered it an honor to be there. He wasn't sure how a woman like her found herself in the present situation, but he was glad he was there at the same time.

Even though Rebecca knew he had paid for her and she was at his mercy, she felt a strange aura of respect and consideration from the odd man touching her. He was much cleaner than she thought he would be and the Old Spice helped considerably. It did feel good and she did need a place to stay. She had no idea who Julius Thurber really was.

Julius Thurber was considered a notorious serial killer who was supposed to be executed a few years before. He once referred to himself as being an abomination on the earth against his fellow man. He was a career criminal with rape and murder in his repertoire of crimes. It was written in the national newspapers that he had been put to death for a killing spree that stretched over ten states, but he was actually only responsible for three of the twelve deaths during that period of time. Once they started counting the victims, his name kept rising to the top. The newspaper report was incorrect, because he had actually escaped from the Chattahoochee Mental Hospital after he did what he considered a good deed and killed the young homosexual orderly who had broken both Julius' wrists and molested Jason.

The authorities could not report they had lost Julius Thurber again. He had escaped three times before, and they just hoped he went far away. He did drop out of sight but wasn't really very far away. He went to the settlement on Black Hammock Island and told his story to Aunt Annie. He had been there ever since. He became part of the Black Hammock family and was one of Aunt Annie's best protectors and fiddler crabs.

CHAPTER TWO

Jason and Theda were sitting on the front porch when Fabian arrived back at home. Theda was nursing her baby, but had her breast covered. Fabian walked up unto the porch. Theda was cool as a cucumber. "I'm glad you didn't leave me alone all this time. You alright?"

Fabian smiled at his little sister. "Damn, Theda. You don't just tell Mary C. 'I gotta go.' You go when she says 'go'." He looked at Jason. "Ain't that right?"

Jason nodded and smiled. Fabian sat down next to Theda and the baby. He looked at his fifteen-year-old sister. "I can't believe my baby sister's got a baby of her own. A baby havin' a baby." Theda ignored his comment. Fabian looked at Jason. "She been borin' you with all her foolish talk?"

Jason looked at Theda and gave a half smile. "She's been just fine."

Rebecca Milkduds Esmeralda Coolie was sitting on top of Julius Quasimodo Thurber. He was mesmerized as he looked up at her young incredible body. She pushed her hips down and whispered "Oh, Daddy" as her stomach muscles contracted and she released her sexual fluids. Julius moaned and pushed his hips upward with one last drive deep inside her. They both experienced that rare and elusive, but sought after, simultaneous orgasm. They did not hear the first knock on the bedroom door. They did hear the second heavy knock and Aunt Annie's crude voice.

"Time's up, lover boy. Playtime's over. Get your big ass back to work."

Julius placed his hands on both sides of Rebecca's hips and rolled her gently off his body and to the side. He picked his pants up off of the floor and opened the door. Aunt Annie's body filled the doorway. She was grinning like a baboon.

"She's somethin' ain't she? Time to go to work so you can make some more money."

Julius reached into the pocket of his pants and pulled out a fist full of money. He pushed the cash into Aunt Annie's hand. "Add this to the clock and leave us alone." He slammed the door shut and went back to his Esmeralda. Aunt Annie smiled as she walked away from the door and stuffed the money into her pants pocket.

Fabian, Jason and Theda all looked out into the front yard to see a red Corvette rolling in their direction. Fabian failed to mention the fact that Mary C. was coming. "Oh, I forgot to tell y'all she was comin' over. She wants to talk to you, Theda. We've got to find Rebecca, so tell her what you know. And don't even think about startin' any of that secret sister crap. That went out the window when she run off like she did. Tell Mary C. what you know and that's the end of it."

Theda moved the baby from her breast and buttoned her shirt. She was hoping not to show how nervous she was, but that would be impossible. She was only fifteen, and facing Mary C. was an ordeal no one of any age wanted to deal with. Mary C. stepped out of the car and walked up to the porch. None of them spoke. They knew Mary C. would start the conversation.

"Don't y'all look comfortable up on this porch?" She looked directly at Theda. The young girl's heart raced in her chest. "I don't have a lot of time, Theda, so I hope this won't take too long."

Margie hated her day cleaning and working at the store. She sat on her bed holding the white doily she had soiled and taken from Mr. King's haunted house after she and Jason had indulged in anal penetration. She would look for the opportunity to return it and hoped the ghosts hadn't told Mr. King of her theft.

The carousel music box was on the night stand next to her bed. Margie needed to get away from her thoughts. She wanted to run away, but she had already done that. She was back at home with her mother and sisters and her time away from home felt like a crazy dream that never really happened. And even though her experiences at the Giant's Motel were wild, unusual and sexual, Margie was still locked in to the life she hated in Mayport. She knew the magic of the box would take her somewhere, anywhere; good or bad, she did not care. She was addicted to the sexual dreams. It was her way of being defiant and stepping out of the cracker box she found herself in each day. Margie reached for the carousel.

Mary C. was at the wheel of the fire engine red Corvette as she drove off of the Mayport ferry on the Fort George side of the St. Johns River. She turned the car to the left and pushed down the gas pedal. The red rocket was flying on the road toward an area of the county called Oceanway, the only way to get to Black Hammock Island.

Theda Moore had given Mary C. all the information she needed. Mary C. was confident that traveling alone was the best way to handle the situation at hand. The radio was blaring with the instrumental "Green Onions," one of Mary C.'s favorite tunes. It seemed appropriate. Her weapon of choice, a pump action shotgun, was loaded and in the trunk of the car. And needless to say, Mary C. had real class. She was dressed to kill.

Officers Boos and Short stood in the shadow of the Mayport lighthouse in Mr. Greenlaw's backyard. They were standing next to five chicken wire cages. Each cage contained a big rooster--a big fighting rooster. Mr. Greenlaw walked out of his house to see why two uniformed police officers were standing near his prize roosters.

"Afternoon, gentlemen. Can I help you boys in some way?"

Officer Boos was first. "Big birds."

Mr. Greenlaw smiled. "Ain't they, though? Ain't no law against havin' big healthy roosters is there?"

Officer Short was next. "Mr. Greenlaw, we're not here to argue about what these roosters are for. We all know the truth. We want to know why you're not participating in Fight Week on Black Hammock Island?"

"I don't think I know what ya mean. What is that?"

Officer Boos surprised and scared Mr. Greenlaw when he pushed him to the ground, pulled out his pistol and placed the short barrel of the gun on his head. "We don't have time for these word games. I don't think I'll have to shoot you, but if I pull this trigger this close to your ear you'll have a wound that won't be seen. How come you're not fightin' your roosters out on the island for Fight Week?"

Mr. Greenlaw was scared to death. The thought of a ruptured ear drum loosened his tongue. "Aunt Annie won't pay me what they're worth. She's gone from top quality birds to whatever costs the least. I've been fightin' in Georgia the last two months. Them Georgia boys at Roads End still appreciate quality birds. Fat ass Annie's gettin' too big for her queer britches. I'm through with that pussy eater."

The music and colorful lights from the carousel filled Margie's bedroom. She was in a deep sleep, but it was her conscious choice to be in such a vulnerable position. Margie knew she was standing in the white sand near the great oak tree. She was surrounded by a thick misty fog and could not see anything ahead of her. She was afraid as she moved slowly. The only thing that gave her the courage to keep moving was the thought of reaching the tree. The fog was heavy and wet, and she could see her bare breasts and nipples through the front of her wet shirt. Moisture dripped off the end of her nose. She did not like the dream at all. There was no color or sound. Her visibility was zero, so she continued her slow pace, hoping the tree would appear above her.

Suddenly the silence was broken. At first, one voice called out, "Margie!" Then a second voice, "Margie!" Then another and another, until the sound of "Margie!" was deafening. She held the palms of her hands against both her ears. As fast as the noise began, it ended. She removed her hands from her ears.

Margie thought perhaps it was the line of sexual partners she had encountered before in her last dream. They were waiting for her and calling to be the first to enter her from behind. The fog began to lift up off of the sand. It was an upward clearing. Branches from the oak tree loomed above her. As the fog cleared she could see the silhouettes of children standing at the trunk of the oak tree. She counted to herself, *one, two, three*, as the fog moved up and away. *Four, five, six, seven, eight.* Eight children stood in the light fog.

She could not see their faces, because the fog around them had only lifted to neck high.

A second look from Margie revealed the children were naked, and a third look told they were all boys with huge male organs hanging down in front of them. A horrible feeling ran through her body when a raspy voice she recognized cracked and caused the fog to be completely gone. Music and color were everywhere.

"We've been waiting for you, Margie!" It was the pervert midget, Tom Thumb, and seven other naked dwarfs. Margie turned to run, but they were on her and took her down like a pride of lions taking down a zebra on the Serengeti. Margie heard Little Tom's crude, evil, nasty voice as the other little people began ripping at her clothes. "Turn her over, boys; she likes it in the butt. She's a Mud Dobber." Before Margie passed out she heard Tom's voice one more time. "Come on Doc, Dopey, get in there. The carousel's about to stop." Margie was sorry she had seen those children's books that day. It was very possible she was being raped and sodomized by Tom Thumb and the seven dwarfs.

The music box stopped spinning. Margie opened her eyes and was more than happy the strange dream was over. She was naked and dripping wet. She looked for white sand in the bed and on the floor, but all was clean. After, all, it was just another crazy dream. *Damn those children's books!*

With the possibility of grave eardrum injury, Mr. Greenlaw had told the two aggressive police officers all they needed to know about Black Hammock Island. They planned to be part of the Saturday crowd and just make mental notes of any illegal activities they might observe. It was an exciting assignment, and both officers were more than ready to accept the challenge.

The majority of the crowd of spectators turned to watch the red Corvette roll slowly on the dirt road leading to Aunt Annie's main house. Mary C. had the convertible top down so everyone could see her. The word of her arrival had carried to the main house where Aunt Annie and her two lovers stood on the front porch waiting to greet the visitor. There was also a young man standing at the far end of the porch. He was armed with a small sawed off shotgun that was strapped to his side in an open bottomed leather holster. A single belt of shotgun shells crossed his chest. A black handle machete lay against his thigh. He was one of Aunt Annie's true dedicated fiddler crabs. He looked very capable of doing his job. There were usually two armed protectors when new visitors came calling, but Julius Thurber had his big head between Rebecca Coolie's smooth legs at that very moment. Protecting Aunt Annie was the last thing on his sex filled mind.

Mary C. did not see the young man with the gun at first. She stopped the car, but left the motor running and remained seated behind the steering wheel. Aunt Annie smiled and stepped forward, leaving her two companions a few feet behind her.

"Well, I'll be damned. What they say about you is true, Mary C. You don't change at all. That pact you made with the devil must'a done the trick. I hear about ya all the time, but, seein' ya like this sure gives all that talk some real substance." The two companions looked at one another after the "pact-with-the-devil" comment. Mary C. tried to ignore it, but Aunt Annie continued. "Don't act like you don't know what I'm talkin' bout. Miss Anna Jo Hamilton told me there was a strong possibility that you slept with the devil."

Mary C. had a mental flashback of a woman she knew years ago. She turned off the car engine and had to respond. "I ain't heard that name in years. That sounds like somethin' Anna Jo would say. You do know she's been dead for a few years, don't ya?"

Aunt Annie smiled. "Not hardly. She was here last month and she did say that to me. I wanted her to stay and be a fiddler crab. I think the men would have liked her with all that witchcraft stuff. She's still pretty enough and she's still built up good. She's got a little age on her but carries it well. Just like you." She waited for Mary C. to respond, but it did not come. Aunt Annie continued. "I remember when she was wild as they come. You know folks don't really change. Anna Jo had her wild moments and probably still does, but she really never was cut out for this kinda whore work. I think you two are just alike. Y'all can't die yet. I think y'all both slept with the devil. Maybe she didn't mean to. It just happened. But, now you, on the other hand, knew what you was doin'. I don't think either one of y'all's gonna die until the devil comes to collect those black souls y'all sold off. He likes the way you two seem to hand over those lost souls. Anna Jo used her body and spells to send 'em to the devil and you just found the ones going to hell anyway and you killed 'em. Satan's got to love you two, alright. I know Anna Jo's got some strange powers from somewhere. Do you have the same powers? Are y'all both witches? I heard the women in her family were all witches. They say those kinda people pass their powers to the next one. I don't know much about that stuff, but I know it gives me the heebie jeebies." Aunt Annie rubbed her chill bump arms like she was wiping away the heebie jeebies.

Mary C. shook her head. She could not stop the flashes in her head. She focused on Aunt Annie. "Anna Jo died in car accident about three years ago near a place called Providence down state somewhere. She moved away from Mayport about a year before the wreck."

Aunt Annie grinned. "Well, I beg to differ with ya on that point 'cause she sat right here on this porch and talked with me all afternoon. She was full of her dreams and came to tell me what I needed to do to be saved from the depths of hell. Ain't that a kick in the ass, a damn witch tellin' me I'm doin' wrong and tryin' to save my sinful soul? I thought witches just took souls. Hell, it was probably a trick of some kind to get me to sell my soul like y'all did."

Mary C. took a deep breath and got out of the car. She had to comment on Aunt Annie's thoughts. "Anna Jo always had a few tricks and treats for the ones she wanted to get somethin' from. To answer your question, I ain't got no powers to do nothin'. And we all know Anna Jo practiced witchcraft, but I have to say I really never saw her hurt nobody. Folks just seemed to go in her direction, especially the men. You make it sound like she flew around on a damn broom, eatin' children and castin' magic spells on folks. Anna Jo got caught up in all that black magic and witchcraft as a family thing, just like some folks grow up in a religion of some kind. It was her religion."

Aunt Annie interrupted. "You seem to be defendin' our little evil witch."

Mary C. tried not to show her temper. She wanted to tell Aunt Annie what an idiot she was, but that would be a mistake at that moment. Perhaps she would tell her at another more appropriate time.

"We all liked Anna Jo. John was crazy about her."

Aunt Annie jumped in again. "Them damn love potions. Hell, John probably didn't need one, crazy as he is."

Mary C. shook her head. "Anna Jo started scarin' everybody with her black magic preachin'. It even got worse when Anna Jo hooked up with Aunt Matilda. With her one black eye seein' the future, her form of witch doctorin' fit right in with Anna's carryin' on."

Aunt Annie had not heard about Anna Jo's visit to Aunt Matilda's Place. She was more than curious. "What did Aunt Matilda tell her?"

Mary C. hesitated for a few seconds, took a deep breath and looked into Aunt Annie's bloodshot eyes. "I don't know what they talked about. I do know that after she was out there, she left Mayport. With Aunt Matilda gone, we'll never know what was said. Anna Jo got kinda scary before she left."

"Anna Jo don't scare you, does she? Nothin' scares you."

"I've been scared before."

Aunt Annie changed the subject. "You been known to cook up a potion now and then, ain't ya? A little witch's brew, maybe? Probably one of them 'love' potions. I can't believe you get all those men to look your way with just your charmin' personality. As you get older you must need a little help now and then."

"I ain't never cooked up no potion; love or any kind." Mary C. had to smile and added some information for Aunt Annie to chew on. "Wait a minute. I might have made a love potion one time." Aunt Annie was all ears. "One morning Aunt Matilda sent Zulmary to my house and asked me to pee in a Mason jar. I think she added it to a love potion."

Aunt Annie wrinkled her manly face. "Zulmary gave me a love potion when she stayed here for a few days a while back. She was on the run. Boy, did she earn her keep. As long as I could keep her mouth shut the men loved her. She talks some crazy lingo, don't she? I was hopin' she'd stay and become a real bonified fiddler crab, but I woke up one mornin' and she was gone. She burned down her mama's store, ya know. With her mama in it. Her mama was already dead." Aunt Annie was silent for a moment. "I like Zulmary. I liked her mama, too." She looked at Mary C. "You really peed in a jar for Aunt Matilda?"

"Sure did. Aunt Matilda sent word she needed my body juices to make a love potion."

Aunt Annie took a deep breath. "I'm glad I ain't used that potion yet."

Mary C. turned away from Aunt Annie and had to smile. She was glad the subject had changed. "I like Zulmary, too. I wish she would have stayed in Mayport, but I guess she got too scared."

Aunt Annie had more thoughts about Mary C.'s strangeness. "Let's see now, your one and only friend lives in a haunted house. I heard you moved in with his crazy ass. They say that boy of yours is a real oak baby, and he belongs to that evil oak tree as much as he belongs to you, meanin' you had to spread ya legs under its branches about twenty years ago." Aunt Annie's two companions were also all ears as she continued. Mary C. just listened, too. "You killed Johnny D. Bryant and they say some other men. He thought he was the devil, but you had to show him who the real devil was. Johnny D. brought some bad ass dogs out here to the island. I don't think they ever lost a fight. He made me a lot of money with them damn wild dogs. Ya kinda got into my business when ya had to kill that crazy bastard."

Mary C. knew she had to hold her own with the king-queen of Black Hammock Island. "Actually, you never crossed my mind when I stuck that shotgun in his mouth."

"No, I'm sure I didn't. They say you killed all his dogs, but one and that hound from hell is your protector as we speak." Aunt Annie looked around. "He ain't gonna run up here on my porch and eat me when I ain't lookin' is he?"

Mary C. shook her head. "The dog's dead by my hand."

Aunt Annie's eyes lit up. "He crossed ya, didn't he? Can't cross the devil, can ya?" She turned to her two companions. "You hear me? You cannot cross the devil. I don't know how ya killed 'ol fat Macadoo and got away with it. Now, don't get me wrong, if any fat black pig needed killin' it was Macadoo. Preachin' Jesus durin' the day and dancin' with the devil at night. She did need killin'. I just want you to tell me how the hell ya did it."

"The law said Tom Green killed Macadoo. They even hunted him for the murder."

"What about our home town voodoo woman, Voo Swar? Tom Green kill her, too?"

Mary C. looked past Aunt Annie at the other two women listening. She looked into Crew Cut's eyes.

"No, I killed her. She came to my house to kill me and take my grandchild so I killed her. Splattered that head scarf full of roots all over the place."

Aunt Annie smiled again. "I was waiting to see if you was gonna tell me about that or not. I already knew the truth. Anna Jo told me about Voo Swar. She also said you killed Eve when she came back. Now that was a real witch there, but I still liked Eve. Folks say Eve cast a spell on a priest and he became her sex slave. He even tattooed his body in her honor. If that don't sound like castin' spells, I don't know what does. Why ya had to kill Eve?"

"I didn't kill Eve. She left town."

"Anna Jo said she saw you burn Eve in a dream. She also told me that grandbaby of yours is the purest of the oak babies. I guess that means somethin' to the oak tree people. It's all creepy to me, but, hell, what do I know?"

Mary C. was tired of the subject matter. She had only tolerated it because she knew if she challenged Aunt Annie it would jeopardize her real mission. She looked up at Aunt Annie standing above her on the porch. "Next time you talk to Anna Jo, tell her to come see me, but in the meantime tell her she can kiss my ass."

"I didn't mean to ruffle them pretty feathers of yours, Mary C."

"Yes you did, Annie."

"Yeah, I guess I did. I'm just messin' with ya. I do like Anna Jo, though. I'd rather have her for a friend than an enemy. I sure didn't know how much you liked Anna Jo. I didn't know you ever had a real female friend. Hell, Mary C., I'd rather have you for a friend than an enemy, too. I ain't never been too sure where we stand on that."

Mary C. did not respond, but had a question. "What was Anna Jo doin' here anyway?"

Aunt Annie smiled. "That's pretty interestin'. Seems like I kept showin' up in Anna Jo's dreams, just walkin' round like I knew I was there. She had dreams about you, too. She come here to ask me to change my ways and to warn me that my punishment would be soon and harsh. That's her word, 'harsh'. Not too scary, but that's what she said. You'd think a damn witch would use a better word then 'harsh'." Aunt Annie changed the subject again. "This has turned into the best Fight Week ever. First, my long, lost niece comes a callin' and now you."

Mary C.'s usually calm heart raced in her beautiful chest when she realized Rebecca Coolie was somewhere nearby. Mary C. was gifted and she knew things. Aunt Annie looked back at her two lovers.

"We're standing in the presence of greatness." She turned back to Mary C. "You must'a really done somethin' bad to come out this way. You need a place to hide?"

Mary C. smiled. "Now, do I look like I'm hidin', Annie?"

"No, I guess not. Actually, you look like you're doin' pretty damn good, unless you just stole that car. But, I don't think that's true, either. Hell, woman, as many people as you've killed and you still don't need to hide, you are a legend around this place. Something or somebody protects you. Maybe it is that damn oak tree. What do we owe this honor?"

Mary C. knew Aunt Annie's respectful words had a slight sarcastic tone. She inched toward the steps of the porch, wearing a short black skirt, showing her muscular legs and a light sleeveless pullover sweater that made her breasts look even bigger than they were. Mary C. walked onto the porch to stand with Aunt Annie. The young armed guard stepped up to stop Mary C. from getting close to Aunt Annie. Mary C. stopped when she realized he was one of her protectors. Aunt Annie's voice cracked in the air.

"I can't be too careful, Mary C., and you know that. It looks pretty strange you comin' to my island out of the blue like this. I piss a lot of folks off, so please understand. I mean no disrespect, but I gotta be sure you ain't here to hurt ol' Aunt Annie." Mary C. stepped back away from the young man and looked into his eyes as Aunt Annie continued. "Now, you ain't got many places to hide stuff wearin' that skimpy little outfit, so it'll be over in a second or two."

Mary C. knew she was going to be searched for a concealed weapon. The young man had big, beautiful, strong eyes as he stared at Mary C. He was about Jason's age and he had long sandy blonde hair that touched his shoulders. Mary C. knew his face once she zeroed in on his features. No name came to mind, but she had seen him before. Aunt Annie's raspy voice ended her thoughts about the young man.

"I'm sorry, but we're gonna have to pat ya down." Aunt Annie motioned for Crew Cut to do the honors. Mary C. had her own thoughts.

"I'd like him to do it." She stared at the young man. Crew Cut stopped dead in her tracks.

Aunt Annie shook her big head. "You are really somethin' else, Mary C. Pickin' who gets to frisk ya. You are a mess, girl."

"Well, if I have to let somebody feel me up, I'd rather it be him." She looked at Crew Cut with cold eyes. "At least let me enjoy myself." If looks could kill, Mary C. would have dropped dead that very moment. Crew Cut was red with hate and embarrassment.

Aunt Annie nodded to the young man as Crew Cut stepped back and away, staring at Mary C. as she moved. Mary C. could see he was surprised at her request. Only Mary C. saw his upper lip quiver when he stepped to her. She stood still as he checked her front pockets, then he touched her buttocks as he put his hands into her back pockets. Mary C. could feel his nervous hands shaking. Aunt Annie's voice cracked again.

"Check them titties. I don't remember her bein' that big. She might have a bomb in her bra." Aunt Annie and Blondie smiled, but Crew Cut did not.

Mary C. looked up at Aunt Annie. "Ain't wearin' one."

The young man hesitated. Aunt Annie instructed him again. "I said check them titties."

Mary C. stood still as the young man touched and squeezed her breasts one at a time with the same hand." When he moved his hands away, Aunt Annie's voice cracked again. "Now, check between her legs, so I can show her around the place."

The young man laid the palm of his hand against the front of her short skirt. He rubbed up and down and then moved his hand away. He turned back to Aunt Annie.

"She's clean."

Aunt Annie smiled. "Now, you really don't know that for sure, but you do know she ain't got no weapon hidin' somewhere.

Cleanliness is next to Godliness. She's far away from that. Welcome to Black Hammock Island, Mary C."

Mary C. stepped up onto the porch. Aunt Annie's manly frame towered above her. The young man moved back to his guard position at the far end of the porch. Blondie and Crew Cut were puzzled when Aunt Annie did not give her signature grizzly bear hug to her new guest. Mary C. looked up at the tall, man-like Aunt Annie.

"You ain't changed much yaself, Annie."

Aunt Annie smiled. "Now, I never thought you told any lies Mary C., but you and me both know that ain't the truth. You sure gave that boy a thrill, didn't ya? Come on up here and sit with us and tell me what brings you to my little island."

Mary C. did not sit down. She had already wasted too much time. She got straight to the point of her visit. "I need to talk to your niece, Rebecca. She stole somethin' from me, and I want it back. I don't want no trouble, and she can stay out here all she wants. I just want what's mine back."

Aunt Annie's face took on a serious look. "She said her brothers are dead and my brother, Earnest, too. You know anything 'bout that?"

"Hell, I know all about it. She's been stayin' in Mayport ever since it happened."

"Stayin' where?"

"I just want to get what she took. You can ask her about where she's been. It ain't my place to say."

"I understand you not bein' a "teller", but if you come here accusin' my kin of stealin' from ya, don't ya think I need to know a little more than what you're givin' me?"

Mary C. looked at the two companions. Aunt Annie understood. "Come on in the house and we can talk. It sure is good to see ya." Mary C. followed Aunt Annie into the house. "Don't be mad about the witchcraft talk. I was just pullin' your chain."

Big Joe Croom sat in the bar called the Gasser. It was located to the left of Mr. Leek's dock near the main street in Mayport. It was a small cinder block building with a bar, a few tables and a small dance area if a Mayport woman wanted to get a man fighting over her. The bar was notorious for the fights that occurred on a nightly basis, but it always seemed to have customers. Early in the evening, it was a pleasant place to sit and have a drink with a friend, but as it got later each night the amount of alcohol consumed seemed to change the personalities of the patrons. Joe Croom sat alone at the bar. He was sad, depressed and wanted to sit there and have a drink while he considered his situation with his wife, Stella. A drink or two might create the answer to his mental dilemma. Three or four drinks might just help him forget the whole thing for a while.

Mary C. and Aunt Annie sat across from each other at the kitchen table. They were drinking iced tea. Aunt Annie was talking. "I need to ask you one more question. You probably ain't gonna like it, but I just gotta know."

"That ain't never stopped ya before, Annie. What is it?"

"Well, ya seem to be takin' out my best customers."

"I'm not sure what ya mean. What customers?"

"Don't get mad, but Anna Jo said you killed Moochie and maybe Junior Price. She wasn't too sure about Junior, but Moochie was definite. Now, they ain't been around in a long time and nobody's seen 'em no where. I think Anna Jo was right. If them two boys wasn't dead, they'd be here right now, tryin' to sell me somethin'. Did you kill 'em?"

"If you started takin' stock in Anna Jo's rantins, then you already think I did it. Not much I can say to change your mind."

"You can tell me if ya did."

Mary C. shook her head. "I shot Moochie in his right ear with my shotgun, but I don't know what happened to Junior."

Aunt Annie smiled. "She was right, then."

"I guess so."

"Aunt Annie had gotten what she wanted. It was time to discuss her niece. "Now, Mary C., you know I want to help ya, but she is my niece and she did come here for my help and protection. You of all people understand how you take care of your own blood, no matter what."

"Like I said, she can stay out here for good. I ain't never gonna tell a livin' soul where she is, but she's got somethin' that's mine."

"I believe you about not tellin'. I would never dispute your given word. But, I need to know more. You gotta give me that."

"What about us both talkin' to her together. You'll catch her in a lot of big lies, but maybe with me here, she'll just tell the truth and get it over with. Then, you can make a decision on what to do."

Aunt Annie nodded and smiled. "Damn, Mary C., you're really sure of ya self, ain't ya?"

"Just get her in here."

"Well, that ain't possible right now, cause she's gonna be busy for about another hour, but when she's free, the three of us will sit down right here and get this thing settled. Now, while we're waitin', how 'bout me showin' you some of the action goin' on around here? A woman like you will appreciate what I've built on my little island."

Mary C. did not want to linger, but she knew she was at Aunt Annie's mercy. She followed she-man back to the front porch. Crew Cut and Blondie were both still sitting together. Blondie smiled at them, but Crew Cut did not. Aunt Annie smiled, too.

"I don't think my friend likes you very much, Mary C. But, you don't care, do ya?"

Mary C. did not look at Crew Cut as she stepped off the porch. "Yeah, I get that a lot. I got too many friends as it is. I don't need no more."

"Hell, Mary C., you ain't got no friends. Well, maybe one. But, he's looney as they come."

"Come on, Annie, ya gotta like John."

"I like Mr. King, but he is a crazy bird."

"Hell, Annie, we're all crazy."

Aunt Annie nodded. "Ain't that the truth."

A loud cheer from a crowd of spectators took their attention away from the porch. A long black hearse was driving slowly through the people. Mary C. thought about Mr. John King's former favorite means of transportation, but she knew he had not followed her to Black Hammock Island. Aunt Annie could not see who was driving the chariot of death, but she knew who it was.

"Oh, my God! He's come in early. He's gonna stay the night. I really am gonna cum in my pants." The Grave Digger had arrived.

The black hearse stopped when Aunt Annie stepped out into the dirt road. The engine went dead as the driver's side door opened and the biggest, ugliest man either woman had ever seen stepped out of the car. The crowd exploded with yelling and cheering as he just seemed to keep getting out. Like Aunt Annie had said, "He was a monster of a man."

Grave Digger wore black sweat pants with black converse tennis shoes. A black tank shirt accented his muscular physique. His massive granite, boulder-like chest tapered down to a thirty-inch waist. He was a truly amazing specimen. He was also the ugliest man anyone standing there had ever seen.

His head was shaved but distorted by knots, bumps and scars. His head was also peeling from too much sun or a skin ailment of some kind. He had a combination horse-hatchet face. It was long but thin and sharp. Grave Digger was an unusual and unpleasing looking individual. The end of his long chin was squared like a concrete cinder block. One eye was a bulging bug-eye, but the other eye was normal-bloodshot, but normal. His Adam's apple protruded beyond normal limits, and it was actually the first noticeable defect. It looked like you could hang a coat hanger on it. Aunt Annie whispered to Mary C.

"Jesus Christ, what the hell is it?"

Mary C. never changed her expression. "You still gonna cum in your pants?"

"I just dried up."

Mary C. had to smile as Aunt Annie turned to see Julius Thurber standing at the front door. Rebecca Coolie was not with him. She turned back to Grave Digger. "Welcome to Black Hammock Island." She did not want to, but Aunt Annie stepped to Grave Digger and shook his hand. He was at least six inches taller than Aunt Annie.

Grave Digger smiled at Aunt Annie, revealing only four teeth in his upper gums and two canine teeth on the bottom. The four uppers had missing teeth between each one. He only had one tooth for every three spaces.

Aunt Annie couldn't take it. She looked away from the awful smile to give instructions to Blondie and Crew Cut. "Take care of our guest. Put him in number five; it's got the biggest bed." She turned back to Grave Digger. "We'll talk later."

Grave Digger nodded to Aunt Annie then grinned at Mary C. She could not help herself. "We won't talk later."

Aunt Annie walked to Julius Thurber as she entered the house. "You had enough, or you got more money for me?" He wanted to tell her how wonderful his two hours had been with his Esmeralda, but he knew better. Aunt Annie knew she would use his newly found weakness against him somewhere down the road. She had more. "You didn't hurt her or nothin' did ya?"

Julius did not like the question. "Of course not. Why you gotta ask me somethin' like that?"

"Is she alive?"

He hated her for asking that question, too. "Stop it, damn it."

Aunt Annie knew by his tone she had touched a nerve. "Well, I got nervous when I remembered that other girl you paid for twice in one day."

Julius' face went red. He talked through clinched teeth. "That was an accident. That won't ever happen again."

"Right, as long as nobody laughs at you in the bed."

"I told you it had nothing to do with her laughin'. It was an accident, and I'd appreciate it if you wouldn't mention it again."

Aunt Annie knew her limits with the serial killer and her best fiddler crab, so she changed the subject. "Well, while you were wallerin' all over my niece, we've had an interesting visitor arrive and Grave Digger's here, too. Remember, you're here to protect me, but Luther took care of everything."

Mary C.'s heart jumped when she realized the young man who checked her for a weapon was Luther Rude, a Mayport boy who was supposed to have drowned at the Big Jetties. He had killed a number of black men while hunting in the woods and then went home and killed his abusive father. His death was considered a suicide. Luther's weapon of choice used to be a hunting bow and arrows, but he had converted to heavy fire power to protect Aunt Annie. Mary C. looked toward the far end of the porch where he had been standing guard, but Luther Rude was gone.

Aunt Annie knocked on the bedroom door. "Comin' in girl. Got a visitor with me."

Aunt Annie opened the door and Mary C. followed her. Rebecca Milkduds Coolie was lying on the striped mattress. But the mattress was on the floor, not the bed frame.

She was completely naked with the stained sheet at her feet. She was on her side with her legs rolled up and the front of her body away from view. Only her back and butt were visible. There was no movement. Aunt Annie had a moment of concern.

"I'll feed that fat pig to the dogs if he's hurt her too bad." She leaned down and touched Rebecca's beautiful shoulder. She rolled over to face her aunt. Rebecca had been sleeping.

"You alright, girl?"

Rebecca focused her eyes on her Aunt Annie. "Oh, I guess I fell asleep."

"He hurt ya?"

"No, I'm fine." Rebecca's big, beautiful eyes focused in on Mary C.'s face. She sat up quickly, like she had been jerked up off of the mattress. She felt her heart pound against her chest. "What's she doin' here? Get her away from me." Rebecca pulled the sheet over her naked body and moved to the corner of the room.

Aunt Annie looked at Mary C. and then back at Rebecca. "You need to talk to me, girl. Mary C.'s been tellin' me some interestin' stuff with you right in the middle as a main character. Rebecca was scared, and Aunt Annie knew it. "You got somethin' that belongs to her?"

"No. She's lyin'."

Mary C. did not move toward Rebecca. "I just told her about you takin' somethin' that belongs to me. I want it back, and you can tell your aunt whatever you want. That's up to you and her. I'll leave you both alone. But, I want it back. If it ain't here, tell me where it is, and I'll go get it. I can't let ya keep it. You knew that when you left with it."

Aunt Annie was going crazy. "What the hell is it?"

Rebecca stepped toward Mary C. "She thinks I stole a diamond necklace. It ain't even hers. But, she's wrong. I don't have it. I never had it. I've never even seen it."

"Like I said, I just want the necklace. Nothin' else matters to me."

Aunt Annie calmed herself. "What makes you think she's got your necklace?"

"First of all, I don't just think it, I know she has it. Her brothers actually took it from my house, but when they got killed, she knew where it was. She ran because she's got it."

Rebecca shook her beautiful head and looked down at the floor. Mary C. had caught her in a very awkward situation, and she was not prepared for such a confrontation. Rebecca Coolie had no time to get her wits about her. Mary C. had the upper hand.

Aunt Annie was becoming more interested. "This necklace worth a lot of money?"

"It has sentimental value to me, but it is worth some money to whoever has it."

Mary C. knew Rebecca could not tell Aunt Annie about the true worth and value of Miss Stark's necklace, or she would lose it for good to her thieving money-hungry relative. Rebecca knew Mary C. had her by the throat. She made a last ditch effort.

"Do what you want. I don't have it."

Aunt Annie shrugged her big manly shoulders. "Well, Mary C., I don't know what to tell ya. She says she ain't got it. Ain't never had it. We're kinda at a deadlock here, ain't we?" She looked at Rebecca. "I hope you ain't come here today with a pocket full of lies. I won't tolerate lies."

Mary C. walked out onto the front porch. The sun was going down, and Friday night on Black Hammock Island was an hour away. Aunt Annie had an idea. "Mary C., just so there ain't no hard feelins, why don't ya stay the night and have a little fun on my island? You can listen to music, drink a little, dance, play cards, and roll some dice. Hell, I'll even have my boy Luther finish what you started today on the porch. That was a classic--you choosin' who patted ya down. I won't forget that one for a long time."

Mary C. had no intentions of stayin' on that hell hole island overnight. She even thought about driving away and coming back during the night with her shotgun. Mary C. was weighing her few options when a black pickup truck drove up to the front porch where she was standing. The truck stopped and a man stepped out onto the ground. He was a big man, but not as big as Grave Digger. When he stepped around the front of the truck and came into full view, Mary C. felt her heart actually stop beating for a second. He looked a lot like Hawk. The man's hair was shoulder length and combed straight back with no part on either side. He was not a handsome man, but his face held character and substance. He had the look of a real man. It was what Mary C. thought a man should look like. He did not look exactly like Hawk but his features and the way he carried himself were very close. He could have easily passed as Hawk's younger brother. She knew Hawk had no brothers, but the similarities were uncanny and very disturbing to her.

Aunt Annie smiled and greeted her new visitor. "Can I help you with somethin', mister? You ain't the po-leese are ya?"

He smiled a full mouth of white-teeth smile. "No ma'am, not hardly. I'm Jack Jarvis. I think I'm gonna fight here tomorrow."

Aunt Annie's manly face lit up. "Jesus Christ, you come in early, too. Your opponent has also arrived. I hope y'all don't run into each other. Ain't no money if ya don't fight at noon tomorrow."

"I promise we won't fight tonight. I'd just like a place to sleep. I'll be sure and stay out of everybody's way tonight." He nodded to Mary C. as he moved back to his truck to get his bag. "I need to get my things. Evenin' ma'am."

Mary C. was taken by his appearance and the way he moved. "Evenin', Mr. Jarvis."

He turned back to Mary C. "It's Jack, ma'am. Just call me Jack." He moved to his truck.

Mary C. nodded and turned to Aunt Annie. "I think I'll stay the night, if the offer still holds. I'd like to see that fight tomorrow."

Aunt Annie smiled as Jack Jackal Jarvis followed her into the main house. Mary C. walked in behind them. Aunt Annie turned to her new arrival. "I don't mean no disrespect, but you ain't quite what I expected. I met your opponent earlier and, well, I gotta say I feel a little afraid for ya."

"I thank ya for your motherly concern, but please don't worry about me. I'll give you your money's worth." Mary C. had to smile. She was sure it was the first time Aunt Annie had been considered motherly. Aunt Annie led the way upstairs.

The threesome stopped in the upstairs hallway when Rebecca Milkduds Coolie stepped out of her room. She looked incredible, and she knew it. "Oh hey, y'all. I found these clothes in the closet,

Aunt Annie. I hope you don't mind me wearin' 'em. I just felt like dressin' up and joinin' the party." She looked at Jack Jarvis. "Evenin', mister."

"Evenin', ma'am."

Aunt Annie shook her big head. "This here's Jack Jarvis. He's half of the main event tomorrow."

Rebecca stepped closer to the prize fighter. "Nice to meet ya. When I'm here working, they call me Esmeralda. You don't seem like a fighter."

"Yes, ma'am, I get that a lot."

Aunt Annie interrupted. "This is my smart-ass niece, Rebecca. Pretty, but stupid. But I guess you don't have to be smart when ya look like that, do ya?" She glared at Rebecca. "Your room's down here, Mr. Jarvis." Aunt Annie and Jack Jarvis moved on down the hallway toward his room. Mary C. began to walk with them when Rebecca took her by the arm.

"We need to talk. I know we can work somethin' out without Aunt Annie knowin' anything. You gotta help me get out of here and we'll make a deal. I don't think she's gonna let me leave."

Mary C.'s heart was calm in her chest. "You got the necklace?"

Rebecca hesitated for a second with her head down, then looked into Mary C.'s eyes. "I got it, but it ain't here. I couldn't chance bringin' it here."

Mary C. nodded. "I'll get you out of here. Just be ready to move when I say 'move'."

Rebecca walked toward the stairs. She was dressed in a tight pair of red silk pedal pusher exposing her muscular calves. She wore a halter top that tied under her breasts, showing her stomach. To top off her sexual appeal, she was barefoot and her toe nails were painted the color of Mary C.'s Corvette. Mary C. looked back and smiled as her new partner started down the stairs.

CHAPTER THREE

Jason sat on Mr. King's front porch holding his son, Billy, in his arms. Mr. King joined him. "Your mama comin' home tonight?"

"I don't know. I hope so. Thanks for watchin' Billy today. I know that ain't your favorite thing to do."

"I'm doin' better with it. Seems like I have him at least three times a week. I need to just be ready at all times."

Jason smiled at Mr. King's way of saying things. "Mama *will* put him off on ya, won't she?"

"It's alright, son. If I have to go somewhere the ghosts just take over for me. Hell, they take better care of him than I do. Hope your mama's alright."

The Friday night party on Black Hammock Island was in full swing. The front porch of the main house was filled with people. Music was blaring and women were dancing, some alone and some with partners, both male and female. Rebecca sat on the front porch with Julius Thurber standing near by. He was on guard duty in case any of the revelers got too drunk and out of hand, but he spent most of his time looking at his new love, Esmeralda.

Aunt Annie was slow dancing with Blondie. Her beautiful face was buried against Aunt Annie's huge sagging breasts as they moved slowly across the wooden porch floor. The music was a fast rock-n-roll tempo, but they danced slow while the other dancers moved to the proper beat of the song. Aunt Annie seemed lost in her own world of music and dance.

Mary C. sat on the porch swing watching the activity around her. She was still dressed in her short skirt and sleeveless sweater. She had refused Aunt Annie's offer to choose an outfit from her closet. Mary C. noticed Luther Rude standing at the far end of the porch again. His head was on a swivel as he scanned the area for unwelcome intruders and overzealous dance partners. Mary C. was going to walk over and talk to the former and always strange Mayport boy, but her attention was taken when Jack Jarvis walked out of the main house to join the party. All eyes were on him as he moved through the crowd and stood in front of Mary C.

"I don't think I've sat on a porch swing since I was boy. Is that seat taken?"

"It's all yours, Mr. Jack Jarvis."

"Please ma'am, just Jack."

"What about Jackal? That's a great name."

"I didn't ask for that name."

Mary C. nodded her beautiful head. "Yes ya did. The day you knocked out that first man in front of a crowd of people, you were askin' for such a name. You might not like it, but you asked for it."

Jack Jarvis smiled at his new friend. He liked the way she spoke her mind. "Who the hell are you, ma'am, and what are you doin' in this nasty place?"

"You don't think I belong here?"

"There's somthin' bout ya that just don't fit."

"Well, you're wrong, Jack. If anybody belongs here, it's me."

The song ended, and Aunt Annie noticed Jack Jarvis had joined them. She released her bear hug on Blondie and walked to the porch swing. "Jack, welcome to the party. I didn't think you could stay in your room with all this fun goin' on. Thanks for comin' out. Folks like to be near men like you. Your opponent seems to be more of a gamblin' man then a dancin' man. He's down at the Shed. Can we get ya somethin' to drink?"

Jack smiled. "That would be nice. I'll take one easy Jack and Coke, if you got it."

Mary C.'s eyes lit up as she turned to look at the man who reminded her of Hawk more and more. She thought about how many times she had ordered one easy Jack and Coke.

Aunt Annie smiled. "Now, what kinda place would this be without a supply of Jack Daniels?" She turned to Crew Cut. "Jack and Coke for triple 'J', Jack Jarvis."

Crew Cut did not hesitate to do as Aunt Annie commanded, but it was obvious she did not like being the one who had to serve him. She cut her eyes at Mary C. as she moved away.

Aunt Annie was excited with her guest. "I don't know much about ya, Jack, but if ya like to have a woman before ya fight, I'll get one for ya. No charge, of course. You gonna make me enough money tomorrow. I can get you a free one tonight."

Jack nodded. "I'll keep that generous offer in mind. Thank you. Right now I'd just like to sit in this swing and relax. The music and that Jack and Coke should hit the spot, for now."

Mary C. liked his style. She had a flash in her mind from the past. Mary C. had no idea why she shared her thoughts. "My brother Bobby called Jack Daniels the nectar of the workin' man. He did like his Jack and Coke."

"He's no longer with you?"

"No, he's dead."

"I'm sorry."

"Me too."

Crew Cut arrived with the Jack Daniels and Coke in a short glass. She handed it to Jack Jarvis. He took the glass. "Thank you." He looked at Mary C. "Would you like one, too?" Crew Cut's eyes widened, and she gritted her teeth at the thought of him sending her for another drink. Mary C. smiled and stared at Crew Cut.

"No thanks, I'm just fine. For some reason I don't think mine would taste as good as yours." Crew Cut turned and walked away. She sat down at the far end of the porch where Luther Rude was still standing at his guard post. Crew Cut did not want any more waitress duties. Aunt Annie was slow dancing with Blondie again, even though the song had another up tempo beat.

A yell from the crowd took everyone's attention as Rebecca Coolie joined the dancers. She was wild as she stepped to the middle of the porch. Milkduds Coolie was like a temptress right out of the Bible. She was Salome, Delilah, and Bathsheba all wrapped in a package called Rebecca Milkduds Esmeralda Coolie.

Aunt Annie was wrong. Milkduds Coolie did not need lessons in dancing the Hoochie Coochie. She was the Hoochie Coochie poster girl. She had instinctly created her own unique version of the dirty boogie. It just came natural for the true vixen. It was her gift. All women have a gift; some just don't use theirs. When Aunt Annie saw Rebecca's vulgar and provocative movements and saw the expressions on the faces of the men and women, once again nothing but dollar signs flashed in her head. Her niece was a true sexual treasure, and Aunt Annie knew how to use her talents. Even Aunt Annie had a gift.

Mary C. watched Rebecca but talked to Jack Jarvis. "Miss Coolie has a certain appeal doesn't she?"

He smiled. "Oh, you really think so? I hadn't noticed." They both laughed at his obvious lie. Mary C. liked Jack Jackal Jarvis. She had more thoughts from her past.

She loved Lester Hawk Hawkins in her own way. She enjoyed the "no holds barred" sex with Steve Crane Robertson. She killed Johnny Ax Bryant. Her son Jason was even called "Jetty Man". She never put much credence in those nicknames, but for some reason, her life was full of such men. She ended her unwelcome walk down memory lane and directed her attention to Jack Jarvis. He was taking a drink of his Jack and Coke and watching Rebecca's seductive dance. Mary C. thought of the wonderful belly dancer, Ana Kara. She wondered if Jack Jarvis would take a drink of Jack Daniels before he fought with Grave Digger just to numb any pain he may have to endure. She thought about the classic battle she witnessed between the Jack Daniels Titans, Hawk Hawkins and Big Jake Shackleford. Sitting with Jack Jarvis had ignited buried thoughts. She remembered dancing with Hawk at the Band Shell at Jacksonville Beach. The words came out of her mouth before she could stop them.

"Would you like to dance, Jack?" She wanted to take them back, but it was said.

"Yes, ma'am, I would. I can only slow dance, ma'am. I look real foolish when I start all that jumpin' around."

Mary C. liked Mr. Jarvis. "I only had slow dancing on my mind, Jack. Any other dance with you would be just a waste of my time."

Jack Jarvis thought to himself. *Who the hell are you, woman?* They both stood up and took a page from Aunt Annie's dance lesson book. They danced slow while the music was fast.

No one watched them at first as Milkduds had all the attention. Crew Cut wanted Rebecca. She felt it as the crotch of her white men's skivvies became wet. Julius Thurber wanted Rebecca again as his manliness pushed against his zipper. Aunt Annie wanted Rebecca to keep dancin'. She could see the men on the porch would pay top dollar for a minute with her new Hoochie Coochie girl. She turned to the swing to see if Jack Jarvis was comfortable and having a good time. The swing was empty. She smiled when she saw Mary C. and the Jackal locked together on the porch dance floor. A young pretty girl in her early teens ran up on the porch and whispered in Aunt Annie's ear. Aunt Annie nodded and motioned for Luther Rude to go with the girl. He left his guard post and followed her.

Grave Digger was at the Shed loosing his money at the poker table. He had been guzzling down Wild Turkey like it was Kool-Aid. Most of the usual women who catered to the gamblers in the Shed were staying clear of Grave Digger. He was rude and nasty in every way. Most of the regular players had decided to play elsewhere. Only two other players and the dealer remained at the table with Grave Digger. He looked at the dealer through drunken eyes.

"Nobody cheats Grave Digger." He threw his hand of cards in the dealer's face and reached across the table with his huge hands, pulling the small man up and out of his chair.

Even in his drunken state, Grave Digger knew the feel of the cold steel of a gun barrel. Luther Rude held his sawed off shot gun barrel against Grave Digger's temple. "I hope you don't make me pull this trigger. Aunt Annie wouldn't like me killin' you before your big fight. But, know deep down in your soul, mister, I will splatter your head all over this table if you decide to act crazy with me. Now, let him go, and let's me and you take a walk in the fresh air so you can clear your head. It would be much better for you if you cleared your head instead of loosing it."

Grave Digger released the dealer. "After the fight tomorrow, I'm comin' back for my money." He pushed the table and walked outside with Luther. The gun barrel remained against his head as they moved together. Luther stepped away when they were outside. Grave Digger was drunk and mad. "I won't forget you, either."

"I'm sure you won't, sir. Now, please sit down out here, and I'll get you some coffee." Luther motioned to the young teenage girl. She ran to get the coffee.

Jack Jarvis was a much better dancer than he had led Mary C. to believe. She had danced with great dancers during her life, and she could tell Jack had natural potential to be one of the better matadors on the dance floor. It was fun and exciting for her to be in a man's arms moving to a fun song.

Aunt Annie smiled and shook her head as the two of them looked like they were high school seniors at the prom. The sight of Luther and Grave Digger walking up to the crowded porch took Aunt Annie's attention. Luther held his shotgun at his side. It was not pointed at Grave Digger's head, but it was not in the holster either.

Luther stopped at the steps as Grave Digger walked up onto the porch. When an ugly man is drunk he even looks worse. Grave Digger looked at Aunt Annie. His voice was low and his words slurred. "Y'all can all kiss my ass." He moved past Aunt Annie. He did not notice his opponent as he moved to the front door.

Mary C. looked at Jack as Grave Digger went into the house. "You really gonna fight that monster?"

"I reckon so. I can't very well run away now, can I? What would you think of me?"

"Come on, Jack, we both know there ain't no *run* in you. I've seen men like you my whole life. You like the pain, and you like causing the pain. But, in this particular situation you could do a favor for your opponent."

"And what kinda favor would I even want to do for a man who wants to kill me?

"You could try and knock some of the ugly off his face."

Luther followed Grave Digger but turned to Aunt Annie before he entered the house. "I did manage to get a little coffee in him. I'll tuck him in and stay 'til he's sleepin'."

Aunt Annie nodded.   As Luther moved away she could see Rebecca locked in a slow dance. Aunt Annie's face turned red when she realized Rebecca's slow dance partner was her number one body guard, Julius Thurber. She thought, *My God, the fat fool thinks he's in love.* She did not want to argue with him or cause a scene with all her company present. She would flex her power and dock his wages when the time was right.

Darkness had taken Mayport. Mr. King sat on his front porch with Jason. Billy was asleep in Jason's lap. "I don't have a good feelin' 'bout ya mama bein' this late. I can't put my finger on it, but I don't like my feelin' right now. She was talkin' to Fabian about that girl and that necklace. She left and ain't come back. You think she's alright?"

Jason had information about his mother, but he could not share it with Mr. King. "You know Mama. She'll be here when she gets here."

Jack Jarvis was standing with Mary C. next to the railing at the far end of the porch. "I've sure enjoyed bein' with you this evenin'. In the middle of all this wild hoop-la you seem to maintain an even keel about you. You calm me, and I don't have that feelin' too often or maybe not at all. Anyway, I like it, and I thank you again."

No one had complimented Mary C. in such a way in a long time, if ever. "You're pretty good company yaself."

Jack's next comment took Mary C. by surprise. "I need to maintain a level of discipline if I'm to survive my meeting tomorrow with that handsome devil, Mr. Grave Digger. I need to rest now and prepare myself. The fact that he is drunk right now gives me the advantage and I need to use that knowledge for my benefit. While he's sleepin' it off, I'll be just sleepin'. That's a big difference."

Mary C. had seen men fight better when they were drunk or coming off one, but she did not share her pugilistic experiences with her new friend.

"As much as I would love to spend the rest of the night with you hoping there would be more than dancing and conversation, I have to say good night, and perhaps you'll leave the door open for another time. My daddy had true Seminole blood. He told me how the Indians never laid with their women before they went into battle, because sometime during the fight they would lose the strength in their legs, and it could mean the difference in life and death.

Mary C. had to smile inside. No one had ever told her "Thanks, but no thanks" so eloquently. In fact, she could not remember anyone ever telling her "No thanks" at all. The Seminole Indian story was just too much--period. This Jack Jackal Jarvis was something else. Mary C. wanted to spend more time with him, but her main mission was to get Rebecca Coolie away from Black Hammock Island and retrieve Miss Stark's diamond and ruby necklace.

Aunt Annie pulled Julius Thurber away from his Esmeralda and instructed him to check the Shed for any problems. Mary C. was alone, and she watched Rebecca move away from the porch and stand next to her red Corvette. She joined Rebecca at the car. Rebecca rubbed the door of the car with her hand. "What did you have to do to get a car like this?"

Mary C. smiled. "The way you dance, you could have one tomorrow if you really wanted one."

"You think we can jump into this thing right now and get out of here?"

Mary C.'s heart raced, but she did not change the expression on her face. "I think that's the way we'll do it, but a little later when things are crankin' down. Let's try a midnight run. That always seems like a good time to make a break."

Rebecca nodded her head. "You start the car at midnight, and I'll be sitting next to you ten seconds later."

Aunt Annie watched Rebecca leave Mary C. and walk back into the house. She approached Mary C. "I'm sure glad you decided to stay and watch the fight tomorrow. You made a new friend tonight, but you always did get the real men to look your way, if there is such a thing as a real man. I hope this thing with you and Becky can be over."

"I guess it has to be for now, but she's still lyin'. It's over because I'll respect your authority here, but if I see her on the outside, I will make her tell me the truth."

Aunt Annie changed the harsh subject. "I was thinkin' awhile ago that I didn't set you up in a room for the night. When you told me you decided to stay, the party got started, and I plumb forgot my manners. I just get giddy headed and catawhompus when I start slow dancin'. Come on." Mary C. followed Aunt Annie upstairs to one of the smaller bedrooms, but it was all she needed.

Aunt Annie stood at the door before she left. "I'm surprised and a little disappointed, Mary C. I thought you'd be ridin' that big stallion by now. People gonna think the devil's lost his hold on you. Of course, the night ain't over yet, so there's still hope."

Mary C. was calm and ready for the word bantering. "He wasn't interested. He's some kind of Indian, and he can't screw and fight in the same place or somethin' like that."

Aunt Annie put her head down and rubbed her cheek. "I don't know about that Indian crap, but don't try to tell me he ain't interested. He looked like he was gonna eat you right there on the porch."

The green family station wagon pulled up in front of Mr. King's haunted house. Mr. King and Jason were still sitting there with Billy in Jason's arms. Jason was surprised when he saw Margie driving. Sofia stepped out of the passenger's side door.

"Evening, Mr. King. Hey Jason."

Mr. King responded. "Evenin', Miss Sofia. What brings you two beauties to my house tonight?"

Sofia answered as Margie got out of the car. "We were hoping we could keep Billy tonight and give Miss Mary C. a break. Margie suggested it and I agreed. If that's alright with you, Jason?"

Sofia had no idea how "alright" her offer was. "Mama's not here, but y'all can sure have his little butt."

Sofia walked up the steps and took Billy out of Jason's arms. Margie stepped up onto the porch and stood near the door. "I'll get his things if that's okay?"

Mr. King made a suggestion. "His things are upstairs. I'll get 'em or Jason will if you don't want to go up there."

Margie surprised everyone when she walked through the front door into the haunted house. "I'll get 'em." She had never really been afraid of the house, but just marching in like that was a little strange. Sofia shrugged her perfect shoulders and kissed Billy on his cheek.

Men like Jack Jarvis are always light sleepers. Don't be the one who wakes them up, because you may have to defend yourself.

They spend most of the night waking up over the slightest noise. To sleep three or four hours in a row is a rare blessing but a welcome one. The real men of the world want to go to bed late and wake up early. They cherish every moment. With their lifestyles, each day could very well be their last. Jack Jarvis knew the moment someone opened his bedroom door and walked into his room. No one would ever be able to sneak up on the Jackal.

With one motion he was out of the bed and took the intruder down to the braided rug and the floor next to the bed. He pushed up off the rug with one hand while holding a thin, eight inch blade to Mary C.'s beautiful throat. His eyes were glaring through the dark and his breathing was heavy. Mary C. could feel his and her adrenaline running amuck. She put her hand behind his neck and pulled his lips to hers. The cold blade touched her throat, but he gently pulled it away. Mary C.'s heavy breathing matched his and her hard breasts pushed against his chest. It was one of those erotic moments no one expects, knife and all. Mary C. rolled him over and pinned his arms back to the floor. She couldn't resist.

"The Seminole Indians were stupid. I promise you'll fight harder tomorrow than you've ever fought before."

Margie walked out of the house and joined the others on the front porch. She was carrying a bag with the baby items they would need to take good care of Billy for the night. Margie did not linger and went to the car. "Come on Sofia. Let the men get back to their conversation."

Sofia did not like it, but she said good night to Jason and Mr. King. She took Billy and got into the car. Margie drove away and waved to the two on the porch. Sofia looked at her sister at the steering wheel. "What's up with you? You are the strangest thing sometimes. It was down right rude of you to hurry away like that."

Margie smiled. "I know you're trying to get back with Jason, and I didn't want to watch you make a fool of yourself. You can flirt with him on you own time, not mine."

Mr. King shook his head as the green station wagon moved away. "You never know what you gonna get from those four sisters, do ya? One is as strange as the other. I think that Margie's got the others beat, though. But, they sure are pretty, ain't they?"

Jason had to smile as Mr. King patted him on his back and walked into the house. Jason thought about the instructions his mother had given him before she left. Mr. King walked into his living room and was headed to the kitchen for an early evening cup of coffee. For some reason he looked at the chair that was missing the white doily. He stopped and his heart raced in his chest. The doily was back where it belonged. He smiled and looked around the room. "Thanks, Norman." He did not even think about Margie being in the house alone. He went into the kitchen.

Aunt Annie opened the door to Rebecca's room. She was surprised to see the young beauty alone. "Hell, girl, I figured that fat fool would be tryin' to get a free one. He ain't hiding under the bed is he? Of course he ain't. That was a stupid question. Fat men don't hide under beds."

Mr. King turned from the stove when he heard Jason behind him. "You want some coffee, Jason? Oh, that's right, you don't drink coffee unless you've got buttered toast to dunk into the cup."

Jason smiled at Mr. King remembering his little oddity when it came to coffee. "I need to go see Fabian for a while. We need to make plans about runnin' the boat together."

"Don't worry 'bout me. I got Norman to keep me company. He got the doily back that was gone."

Jason didn't understand for a second. "The doily?"

"Yeah, that white doily on the chair in the living room. It's been missin' all week. I suspected one of our new ghosts was lettin' me know they were here, so I asked Norman to get it back. There it is, right where it's supposed to be." He pointed to the living room.

Jason had a mental flashback of Margie pulling the doily off the arm of the chair and shoving it up her butt. He had to smile at the over-sexed and very cunning Margie.

"I might sleep on the boat tonight, Mr. King."

"As ya mama says, 'I'll see ya when ya get here'." Jason smiled again when he passed by the chair and the white doily.

Jack Jarvis had been with beautiful women before, but he knew none had matched the sexual prowess of the woman working her magic on him at that moment. They were in the bed now, completely naked with their bodies glistening with sweat from the heat they had generated. It was that good sweat when, once again, nothing else matters. Their bodies actually complimented each other with the proper curves and bulges. They were a perfect fit, and Mary C. had to admit to herself that her comfort level was at its highest point. Mary C. liked the way he was able to maneuver her with his strong arms and hands. Most of the men she had shared her body with were strong enough to position her like they wanted. She had always liked that. Jack Jarvis turned her onto her stomach with one motion. Mary C. liked it from behind many years before it became Margie's favorite position. She pushed her butt back toward him as Jack drove deep inside her. There was a slapping noise when their skin started slamming together. Jack realized it was Mary C.'s aggressive and rhythmic pushing that was causing the erotic noise. He stopped moving and allowed her to push as hard as she wanted. He could not help himself. This time he thought out loud. "Who the hell are you?"

Jason drove his truck up to Fabian's front porch. Theda was first to greet him at the door. "I didn't think I'd see you again so soon. You couldn't stay away from me, huh?" She smiled at her own playful humor. Jason surprised her with his unexpected response.

"That ain't too far from the truth. I need to talk to Fabian, but I knew I'd get to see you, and I was happy about that, too."

Theda was floating on air when Fabian walked out to join them. "What's up?"

"Thought we could talk about takin' the boat out in a few days. You ain't beddin' down early are ya?"

"Hell no, I'm wide awake. I'd like to talk about what to do next." He turned to Theda. "Would you mind heatin' up some of that corn beef stew? I know Jason's just like me. He's always hungry."

Theda couldn't wait to serve the two men in her life. "Comin' right up." She nodded and hurried to the kitchen.

When she was out of hearing distance Fabian turned to his friend. "What's the matter? You ain't come back here to talk about the boat."

Jason took a deep breath. "Mama said if she wasn't back by nightfall, she was probably in trouble and she needed help. I was to come get you and for us to go get her. She's out at Black Hammock Island lookin' for the Coolie girl."

Fabian's heart raced. He wanted to be sure Mary C. was safe, but the thought he might see Rebecca Milkduds Coolie added to his desire to go. "Let's go bring your mama back home."

Mary C.'s arms and legs were wrapped around Jack Jarvis' body like Spanish moss wraps around an oak tree limb. She looked up at the big ugly horseshoe clock on the wall. It was almost midnight, and she had a second date to keep with Rebecca Coolie. She tried to stay calm so Jack would not suspect a problem.

"I think I need to go, just in case those Seminole Indians are right about your legs. I'd feel awful if I caused you trouble tomorrow."

Jack smiled. "I thought you said the Indians were stupid."

"Let's just be safe rather than sorry."

"Are you tired of me already?"

She touched his face. "Oh, please don't think that. I just had a lot goin' on before I ran in to your butt. I wasn't 'sposed to stay here tonight. I should have been long gone by now, but you had to show up." Mary C. dressed as she talked. "I live in Mayport. I'm easy to find if you're ever lookin'.'" She kissed him. "It was great. Please don't follow me." Mary C. left the room. Jack honored her last comment and did not follow her.

Theda stepped out of the kitchen to inform her two men the corn beef stew was hot and ready. Her heart jumped in her young chest when she saw her brother Fabian with his combat knife, handgun and pump action shotgun. She knew something was very wrong. She looked at Jason.

"Oh my God, what's happened, now?"

Fabian answered his sister's question. "There a strong possibility Mary C.'s in big trouble. She left instructions for us if she wasn't home by dark. Well, it's dark and she ain't here. We gotta go find her." Theda looked scared. "I'm sorry, but you'll have to stay here alone, 'til we get back. That's just the way it is." Fabian turned away from her and went out into the front yard.

Theda stared at Jason. "Please don't get hurt."

"We won't. We'll be fine."

Mary C. stepped out onto the front porch. The keys to her Corvette were in her hand. She knew she was in deep trouble when she did not see the car. She looked left and then right just in case she was looking in the wrong place. The red rocket was not there.

Mary C. turned back to the screen door when she heard it open behind her. Rebecca Coolie walked through the door. Her heart sank when she saw the car was gone. Before the unlikely duo could speak to one another, Aunt Annie's nasty voice cracked in the heavy midnight air.

"Well, well, ain't you two an unholy pair. I knew y'all was gonna run. Too many looks and whisperin' goin' on. I just know things sometimes. I just might have a little witch in me, too." Aunt Annie stayed in the dark.

Mary C. tried to keep her voice from trembling. "Where's my car?"

Aunt Annie stepped into the moonlight. "Oh, that ain't your car no more. That car was mine right after you stepped out of it. You shoulda left it runnin' and drove off like you planned. It always cost a lot when someone betrays Aunt Annie."

"Keep the damn car. I'll drive Rebecca's truck out."

Aunt Annie stepped up to Mary C. Luther Rude and Julius Thurber flanked her on each side. "I don't think you understand what's happening here, Mary C. You see, this ain't Mayport. When it comes right down to it, you ain't nothin' here."

Aunt Annie hit Mary C. in her face with a closed fist that would have put down any man or woman. The brutal attack surprised all three onlookers. Mary C.'s body went limp, instantly. She was unconscious before her body slammed to the porch floor. Aunt Annie turned to Rebecca and grabbed her throat with one strong hand, pushing her to the side of the house.

"You went against your blood. I have a feeling this ain't the first time. Now, you owe me. You both owe me. I've already seen how you'll pay off your debt. As for Mary C., what better place for her to use her devil given talents than right here on Black Hammock Island."

Theda stood on her front porch. She could see the tail lights on Jason's truck as it drove away. The sound of her baby crying took her attention away from the red lights. At fifteen-years-old, she was already a member of the adult world in Mayport, Florida, U.S.A.

Mary C. opened her eyes to see Luther Rude's face as he laid her in a bed. She closed her eyes from the throbbing pain in her bruised head. Aunt Annie's manly fist had connected with Mary C.'s face right above her right eye. There was a gash about an inch long at her eyebrow with a trickle of blood on the side of her face. She heard Luther's voice in a low whisper. "I'm sorry you got hurt."

Mary C. knew she needed to talk to the former Mayport boy. "Help me get out of here. You can't refuse me. You've hunted in the woods behind my house. You and Joe Croom were best friends. Hell, Luther, you were one of Jimmy Johnston's favorites." He tried to move away, but Mary C. held his arm. "Jason and Fabian will be looking for me. You know my son and Fabian. They know I'm on the island. They won't stop 'til they find me. Help me before somebody dies." He pulled his arm free. Mary C. had more to say as he reached the door. "You do know Joe Croom's dead?"

Luther left the room, and Mary C. realized there was a strap around her ankle and she was chained to the bed. For some reason the room felt different. She knew she was not in the main house.

Aunt Annie walked into the bedroom. Rebecca was afraid. "You really hurt me, girl. Goin' against me like ya did. I think maybe you're too young to understand what blood means."

Rebecca hated what her aunt was saying. "If understandin' blood means livin' like I've had to live, then blood don't mean nothin'. I don't want to stay here. Please let me go." Rebecca was chained to the bed, too.

Aunt Annie sat on the bed next to Rebecca. "Do you know how much money you're gonna make for me during your stay here?"

"Is that the way you treat your blood?"

"You came here for my protection. You'll have to pay for that and the fact you have betrayed and embarrassed me in front of my friends. Get ready to spread them pretty legs, open that mouth of yours and relax that ass-hole. I'll tell ya when your debt's paid. At least I'll let you walk out of here one day. Your friend Mary C. will make me some money, but she will never leave. I will bury her on this island."

CHAPTER FOUR

Jason and Fabian sat in the truck as the ferry carried them to the Fort George side of the St. Johns River. Fabian sat in the passenger's seat loading his pump action shotgun. A duffle bad filled with weapons lay on the floor at his feet. "This will have to be just like before. Hit quick and get out. You do realize we're goin' in blind again? It worked out last time, but they were idiots. This place may be a little more organized."

They were interrupted by one of the ferry workers when he came to the window to collect the fifty-cent fare. Jason handed him the money. The man smiled and looked at Fabian's shotgun. "You boys goin' huntin' tonight?"

Fabian smiled. "They say game's running out on Black Hammock Island. Thought we'd take a look. And be there in the mornin'."

The man smiled. "You boys can't hunt on the island this week. It's Fight Week. You can pay to see the fights--fowl, animal or man--but you ain't doin' no huntin'.

Fabian was curious. "Who fights out there?"

The man was happy to have a conversation and happy he had the answers. "They fight roosters and dogs durin' the week, and tomorrow everybody's gonna be there to see Grave Digger square up with the Jackal. I'm gonna go in and roll some dice in the mornin' and be ringside at high-noon. If you don't do no huntin', that fight's gonna be history in the makin'. I ain't missin' it."

"Can anybody go watch?"

"They pretty open out there lately as long as you don't cause no trouble. You got the ten dollars, you can watch it. They'll collect it from ya when ya drive in. Just have your money ready."

Aunt Annie walked into the room where Mary C. was chained to a bed. Crew Cut and Blondie walked in behind their mistress and master. Aunt Annie walked to the bed. The other two stayed back.

"You know what really pisses me off?" Mary C. knew Aunt Annie was not wanting her to answer. She had her own answer. "The way you came in here and treated me with such disrespect. You actually thought you would walk in, accuse my blood of stealin' and I was gonna give her to ya, just like that." Aunt Annie smiled and changed her train of thought. "I'm sure you've figured out by now, you ain't back at the house. This is our special place for whores and witches who need to be humbled and remember their places. You can yell all you want, but nobody'll hear ya. If by chance somebody does hear ya, they won't care, cause there's noises and screams comin' from these rooms all the time." Aunt Annie looked back at her two lovers. "They gonna be payin' top dollar to crawl in and out of that bed with a legend. I got a little somethin' for ya so you won't remember much of anything. I can't have you gettin' brave and crazy on me and bitin' one of those big porks off one of our customers when he shoves it in your disrespectful mouth. Despair causes folks to go plumb crazy sometimes. I've seen my share of it right here on the island. A woman has just a few weeks left here, and she goes insane with despair, and we have to put her down. It just breaks my heart when that happens."

Aunt Annie motioned to her two companions to come to the bed. They grabbed Mary C. so she could not fight or kick. Aunt Annie joined the others and held Mary C. down, sticking a hypodermic needle into her arm. Within seconds they no longer had to hold Mary C. Aunt Annie moved her face to within an inch of Mary C.'s face.

"You'll be so happy to open them legs in about thirty seconds." Mary C. spit at Aunt Annie's face, but she did not know if it hit her.

It actually did hit Aunt Annie in her left eye. She slapped Mary C. in her face, but she would never feel it or know it.

Jason drove his truck past the gate leading to Black Hammock Island. He drove about a mile down the road before he stopped and pulled off into the woods. Fabian was thinking out loud. "I wonder if we should try to sneak in and find her, or should we go in as customers waitin' for the fight tomorrow?"

Jack Jarvis could not sleep. The clock on the wall read one o'clock. Mary C. had left him over an hour ago. He looked out the upper bedroom window, and he could see a few remaining men and women milling around in the dark. There was no music, but he could hear laughter every now and then. It really wasn't the reason he could not sleep; it was Mary C. and her sudden exit.

Jason and Fabian had made their plan and decision. Fabian pushed open the gate on the road to Black Hammock Island. They would try to become part of the Fight Week festivities.

Mary C. was conscious, but could not lift her head off the bed. The door opened and two figures walked into the dark room. She knew Aunt Annie's voice, but Mary C. could not talk. "You get to start payin' off your debt right now. I knew if I found my good 'ol Woodbine, Georgia buddy here, he would pay to be with a devil like you. Mary C., this is Screwy Louie. I think his name has two different meanings, but you'll see that soon enough." Aunt Annie sat down in a chair near the bed, and Screwy Louie crawled in on top of Mary C. She could only see smiling green teeth, and the smell of moonshine filled her nostrils.

There were moments when Mary C. would be able to open her eyes, and she would see and feel the vile things being done to her, but she did not have the strength or ability to stop them. She mentally moved in and out of consciousness. Most of it was like a bad dream. Mary C. was one of the lucky ones and had never had many dreams at all in her life; good or bad. If she did survive her current ordeal she would be able to treat it as a nightmare and not reality. At one time Aunt Annie joined in on the sexual abuse, and Mary C. did hear Aunt Annie's awful voice. "Don't act like you ain't never slept with the devil before." Mary C. tried to focus her eyes, but Screwy Louie's nasty face appeared in front of her.

As Jason drove his truck up to the front of the main house, he motioned to Fabian to look to his right. Mary C.'s red Corvette was parked at the side of the house. At least they knew she was still there. None of Aunt Annie's regulars were around. Julius Thurber was asleep in a chair in the hall next to Rebecca's bedroom. Aunt Annie's two companions, Crew Cut and Blondie, were sleeping together, butt naked in Aunt Annie's master bedroom in the main house. Aunt Annie was too involved in her depraved sexual torture of the Mayport legend.

Jack Jarvis stepped out onto the front porch as Jason and Fabian got out of the truck. He was yet to fall asleep, and Mary C. was on his mind. He looked down at the two young men. "Evenin', gents. Kinda late to be gettin' in, ain't it?"

Fabian was a smart young man. "Yes sir. Been drivin' all day. We was hopin' to get to see the fight tomorrow, if all the seats ain't been bought up."

"I'm sure if ya got the money, they got a place for ya. It won't be no ring-side seat, but you might be able to sit up in a tree or somethin'." Jack smiled at his own little joke.

Fabian followed him with his smile. "We'll just sleep in the truck, if that don't break no rules."

"I don't know 'bout no rules, but if you boys don't mind, I got a big room, but the bed's mine. You two are welcome to the chair or the floor if ya can take my snorin'. I ain't no queer man, so don't worry about your virtue."

Fabian smiled again. "We thank ya for such kindness." He motioned to Jason. "Go park the truck out of the way, and let's get some sleep."

Mary C. woke up as the drug began to release its hold on her body and mind. The room was dark, but she knew she was alone. She was still numb, so she would not feel the pain of the abuse until later. Her body tensed when the door to the room opened. She saw one lone figure walking toward the bed. She closed her eyes, so the intruder would think she was still unconscious. A hand touched her forehead first and moved her hair from covering her face. The same hand touched her breasts one at a time, then her bare stomach and thighs. The hand was between her legs with fingers moving in and out of her body. She opened her eyes and looked down. It was Luther Rude.

"Help me, Luther!" Luther jumped up and ran out of the room. Mary C. was alone again. She would have allowed Luther to do his will if he would have just stayed with her. Mary C. was deep into her survival mode, and there was nothing off limits in order to stay alive.

Fabian and Jason could not believe their good fortune as they arranged the rugs and pillows from the chair to create sleeping quarters. Fabian made sure his duffle bag was placed close to him. Jack Jarvis was back in his bed. "I'm not myself tonight, gents. I didn't get your names, and I failed to introduce myself. Please forgive my poor manners."

Fabian was still the talker. "I'm Fabian and this here is Jason."

"Good to meet you boys. I'm Jack--Jack Jarvis. I hope you fellows cheer for me tomorrow. It's always nice to hear some friendly voices in the crowd."

Fabian realized who they were with. Jack Jarvis sat up on the side of the bed. It was a little after two o'clock, and he needed to get some sleep before the big fight. Fabian turned to the bed. "I can't believe we're here with Jack Jarvis." Even though Fabian had only heard about Jack from the man on the ferry, he still acted like he knew of his reputation. "It's an honor, sir. Thank you again for you kindness."

Jack liked the well mannered young man. He had not heard Jason talk yet, but he also liked a man of few words. He confided in the two young men. "I ain't rested good like usual, fella's. It bothers me some, but it's my own damn fault. Damn them women. They'll get us every time. Hell, I almost forgot about the fight when I was with her. It was like she had me under a spell or somethin'."

Fabian smiled. "I've been under one of those spells before. Ain't much you can do about it either." He looked at Jason. "Now, it's backward with Jason here; he puts the spell on the women. They don't put one on him."

Jason shook his head, but did not smile. Jack Jarvis did smile. "Well, I never heard of that, but I sure wish I had the power like that. I'm glad to meet a man like you, Jason."

Jack Jarvis had no idea why, but he wanted to talk about Mary C. "She just walked out of this room a few hours before you boys walked in. She did invite me to come see her. When the fight's over I just might go look her up and see if she really wanted me to pay her a visit. I sure hope so. I've been fishin' in Mayport before and ate at that Strickland's Restaurant, but I ain't never went there to see a woman."

Fabian's face lit up as he turned to face Jason. They both knew Mary C. was the woman Jack was talking about. Neither one knew what to do or say next. They both thought perhaps Jack Jarvis knew where she was and if she was in any danger. It was obvious that Jack thought she was alright, and she had left on her own. Neither one felt Jack had done her any harm. Fabian surprised Jason when he took a chance.

"Your friend's name wouldn't be Mary C. would it, Jack?"

Jack Jarvis had no words for a few seconds. "What's goin' on here, gents? Who are ya?" Jack had a cautious and defensive tone to his voice."

"We came here to find Mary C. We have reason to believe she's in danger and being kept here against her will."

Jack stood up. "How y'all know her?"

Jason spoke for the first time. "She's my mama. She told me if she didn't come home last night for me and Fabian to come get her. She didn't come, so here we are."

Fabian added to the wild story. "If you feel about her like you say, then we have to trust you to help us find out what happened to her."

"You know this looks like I'm bein' set up for somethin', don't ya?"

"It's just the way things are with Mary C. She can make things happen. I'm sure you've already seen that in her."

"Well, she was in a hurry to leave, but she seemed fine. I thought she jumped into the red car and hit the road. You sure she ain't back home lookin' for y'all?"

"We saw the car parked on the other side of the house when we came in. She's still here, alright."

"Why would they want to hold her here?"

"She came lookin' for a girl named Rebecca Coolie. The Coolie girl took something that belongs to Mary C., and she came to get it back. The lady who runs this place is the girl's aunt, and we're pretty sure the aunt would protect her."

"I met her, too. She's here, too."

Fabian looked at Jason. "If Rebecca told her aunt about Mary C., then they did something to her."

Jack Jarvis was concerned, but leery. "This is a lot to swallow. If you boys are on the level, I'm worried for Mary C. There's some bad people around this place."

Luther Rude stood at the door of Mary C.'s room. The windows of the room were covered with black paint allowing no light at all. Only oil lanterns were a source of light if they were lit. She focused her eyes on him as he approached the bed once again. She made sure she got a chance to talk before he got scared again and ran away.

"You can touch me all you want, just stay and talk to me. Don't leave me alone. I don't think you really want them to hurt me, but you know they are. You don't think you can help me, but you can if you make that choice. You know she's gonna kill me when they're through with me."

Luther sat down on the bed next to her. She was still naked. He touched her neck and rubbed her breasts again. He touched the swollen area on her eye. She was tender there, but Mary C. did not show any pain. He stared at her body as he talked.

"I used to see you in Mayport, in the store, at the Little Jetties, on the docks. I had dreams about touching you. As I got older, it got worse. I was just a little boy to you, but I still had those dreams. You know I can't go back there."

"You know you can't let them kill me."

Luther changed the subject. "Tell me about Joe Croom."

Mary C. took a deep breath. He continued to touch her body. "He saved his little brothers from a wild dog, but the dog killed Joe. His funeral was last week."

Luther shook his head. "That sounds like something he'd do. I knew those mean brothers of his were gonna get him killed. He rescued them all the time. I guess Joe's luck just ran out." He bent his head down and sucked on one of her breasts as he squeezed the other one with his hand. He sucked hard and pulled her nipple with his teeth. It was painful for Mary C. after her earlier abuse from Screwie Louie and Aunt Annie. Luther lifted his head. "I heard Jimmy Johnston got killed. He was tryin' to save a boy, too."

Mary C. wanted to keep Luther there with her and talking. "That's right. Jimmy would not want you to let them hurt me."

Julius Thurber had lost what little will power he had left when it came to his Esmeralda. He was afraid of Aunt Annie's evil wrath. He had to see if she was safe or not. He opened the door to her room. Only the light from the hallway shown in the room as the door swung open. She looked to be asleep, so he sat down on the edge of the bed to drink in her beauty. She was naked, and he had a full frontal view of her incredible body. As soon as the weight of his body moved the mattress, Rebecca exploded from the bed and began swinging her arms in a defensive posture. Julius grabbed her arms and pinned them to the bed.

"Stop and be quiet. It's me, Julius." Rebecca's eyes focused in on his face. She stopped fighting. He whispered to her. "Are you alright?"

Rebecca hated his stupid question. "I'm chained to this bed waiting on my insane aunt to sell me piece by piece to the highest bidder. Should I consider that situation as being alright?" Julius hung his head. She was angry. "Don't put your head down. You paid for me first to lead the way for the others."

Julius released his hold on her arms. "I ain't sorry I paid to be with you. You would have never been with me by choice. Men like me don't get that chance too often, if at all. I took the opportunity when it was given. I'd do again the same way."

Rebecca had hate, fear and anger in her beautiful eyes. "So now, you can sit back and let these hogs around here line up at that door and spread my legs whenever they have the money. Hell, you'll be right in line with 'em."

Julius Thurber's heart was betraying him second by second. He was ashamed. It was an emotion he had not felt in a long time, if ever. An eighteen-year-old beauty was causing him to release the strong grip he held on his inner self. Julius was treading on unfamiliar waters and going under fast. Rebecca's voice was all he cared about at the moment. Her words were sweet music to his big, fat, flat ears.

"Take me away from this awful place, before it's too late for us both."

Julius Thurber's heart pounded in his chest. He had never been a fool, but there was a first time for everything. "I've got to take care of a few things before we leave."

Rebecca was scared. She reached for him and grabbed his shirt sleeve. "Let's go now. If you leave me, you won't come back. Aunt Annie will know. Somehow she'll know. Please, let's just go."

He moved to the door. "I'll be right back. I promise."

Rebecca had fear and panic in her eyes. "At least get these chains off my leg. I'll leave them wrapped around it in case someone comes in." Julius stopped and went back to the bed. His heart raced again as he removed the chain. Rebecca's heart was racing, too. "I'll make it look like it's still attached. Now, hurry!"

As soon as Rebecca knew Julius was gone, she was up, out of the bed and putting on her clothes. It did not matter if he returned or not. She was leaving with or without him. Rebecca turned to the door when she heard the doorknob move. She smiled at the thought Julius had returned so quickly to save her. She knew her chances of getting away were much better if he was with her.

Hot liquid filled her throat when two men entered the room. Her big eyes did not focus on their faces at first, but a piercing pain ripped into her heart when she realized Fabian and Jason were standing with her. She actually looked at the bed to see if it was all a dream and perhaps she was still asleep. Fabian's voice told her it was real. His heart was racing, too.

"We're looking for Mary C. Where is she?"

Jason stepped forward holding a hunting knife. "Where is she?"

For some reason Rebecca knew instantly that Jason would not hesitate to use his knife to get the information he wanted. She was a true survivor. "She's somewhere on the island, but I don't know where. We tried to leave together, and they caught us. They brought me up here and chained me to the bed. I don't know where they took her." She looked at Fabian. "That's the truth."

Fabian loved seeing her again, but he could not reveal his weakness. "The truth ain't your specialty, now is it?"

"No it ain't, but you do know what my specialty is, don't ya?"

Jason did not care about the word bantering. He stepped to her side. "I will stick this knife in your throat if I don't hear something worth hearing from you the next time you talk."

Rebecca knew he meant what he said. "The man coming back to take me out of here will know where she is."

Jason looked at Fabian, then back at Rebecca. "When's that gonna happen?"

"Any minute, now."

Fabian pulled his pistol from his belt. "You supposed to be here waiting?"

"Yes. He's helping me get away, but he's one of Aunt Annie's body guards. He'll know where they're keeping Mary C." Fabian motioned for her to sit back on the bed. He moved to the side of the door and Jason moved back into the far corner of the room.

Luther Rude was sucking on one of Mary C.'s breasts and fingering her with a free hand. She made noises of pleasure to keep him interested and with her. He had not taken the chain from around her ankle.

The door to Rebecca's room opened slowly as Julius Thurber had returned to follow his black heart. He smiled when he saw her fully dressed, ready to go and sitting on the bed. He took a few steps toward her before he felt something hit him in the back of the head. He fell to the floor, shaking the entire room with the weight of his body. He was a tough man and did not fall completely into an unconscious state. He rolled onto his back and looked up as Fabian pushed the barrel of his pistol in the big man's face.

"You make one sound and you die. I'll do all the talkin'." Julius Thurber's head began to clear as Fabian continued. "I'm gonna ask you one time and that's all. If I don't get the right answer, you die."

Julius Thurber was not afraid. "You think a man like me's scared of dyin'?"

Rebecca knew if she did not say something, Julius Thurber was surely going to die. "Tell them what they want to know, please. Then we can all get out of here."

Julius looked at his Esmeralda. "What do they want?"

Fabian allowed her to answer. "They're looking for the woman, Mary C. She drove in this morning in the red Corvette, and when she tried to leave, Aunt Annie stopped her and took her somewhere. They came to take her away from here. We can all go."

Julius Thurber looked at Fabian's gun. "You didn't have to hit me like that, mister."

"Oh, no, sir, that was the right call at the moment. Now, where is she? I won't ask you again." Fabian put the end of the gun on Julius' forehead. Jason knew Fabian was going to pull the trigger in a matter of seconds. He had seen that look before. Jason stepped from his place in the room.

"Don't kill him, Fabian."

Fabian held the gun in place. "I've waited too long, now. He ain't gonna tell us. We'll go find her on our own. We can't chance leaving him here."

Jason stepped close to Julius. "He saved my life. I can't be part of killin' him."

Julius Thurber looked up at Jason. He recognized him right away. "Jason, is that you?"

"Yes, sir. They got my mama, and I'm here to take her back home."

Aunt Annie was like a big slab of ham sandwiched between Crew Cut and Blondie. They were all naked and asleep in Aunt Annie's king sized bed with the smell of Slim Jims filling the room. Blondie eased herself out of the bed and wrapped a robe around her naked body. She left the room and went down the hall to the upstairs bathroom. She heard footsteps approaching and hurried to close the bathroom door. She pushed the door ajar so she could see who was walking around at that late hour. Blondie closed the door when she recognized Julius Thurber, but she did not know the man walking with him. She could hear Rebecca Coolie.

"Here's the key to my truck. I'll wait for y'all to come back."

Fabian handed her keys back to her. "Hide in the truck for two minutes, then drive it around front. The more ways for us to leave the better. We might all leave together or in separate vehicles. No tellin' what's gonna happen when this whole thing breaks loose. We might just drive out with no problems, or it could be a life and death situation. Have that truck ready to go. We'll be movin' fast."

The three men moved in one direction, and Blondie opened the door and watched Rebecca walk away in the other direction. Fabian wanted to explain his actions with Rebecca to Jason.

"I know it's a risk with her, but I do think she's tryin' to get out of here. I don't think she'll go tell Aunt Annie we're here. If she stays and waits with the truck, it will give us another option when the time comes. The perfect thing would be to all drive out in both trucks and the Corvette, but that ain't too likely under the circumstances."

After seeing Jason and wanting to help Rebecca, Julius Thurber followed his heart and was going to show them where Mary C. was being held captive. Fabian allowed Julius to lead the way, but he still held his gun in the ready to fire position. He knew a man like Thurber would not forget the blow he took to the back of his head. He had no bones of understanding nor forgiveness in his body. It was in his blood and nature to get even. Jack Jarvis walked next to Jason.

They were outside and moving quickly. They faced no opposition as they moved across the grounds. Julius stopped in front of a row of six tiny square buildings. "She's in one of these, but I don't know which one." He did not move, because he knew Fabian wanted to pull the trigger of that pistol. Fabian was a true born leader.

"It'll damn sure be faster if we all take one." He took the gun off of Julius Thurber. The four men ran to four different buildings.

Jack Jarvis kicked in the door to the one he chose to find three teen aged girls sleeping in a small bed. They were frightened and dirty and huddled together when they saw him enter the room. Julius did not enter one of the rooms. He ran to join Rebecca at the truck. Jason saw Julius run, but finding his mother was the only thing he cared about.

The room Jason entered was empty but smelled like urine and vomit. He stepped back out of the room gagging as he moved. When Fabian slammed through the door to the building he had chosen, he saw the bare back and butt of a man pumping a woman underneath him. Even if it wasn't Mary C., it did not matter to Fabian. He had already waited far too long to kill somebody.

Luther turned as the shattered wood from the door scattered on the floor of the room. He fell to the floor as he dismounted Mary C. and tried to crawl to his gun. Fabian was in his element and comfort zone. His training and ability to kill was much more than Luther Rude could handle. Fabian's combat knife was his weapon of choice at that moment. When Luther saw the flash on the blade in the air, it was too late. The point of the knife entered his body directly below his neck--that spot of soft skin above the sternum. Luther grabbed the handle of the knife with both hands as he lay on the floor. His desire to reach his gun was overshadowed by the pain screaming in his body. Fabian moved to the bed and saw he had found Mary C. She was naked and trying to free her ankle from the dog chain. Fabian lifted the end of the bed and slid the chain off the bottom of the metal leg. Mary C. was free from the bed but would have to remove the chain from her ankle at another time. She turned and wrapped her bruised naked body in the dirty sheet off the bed.

"It took y'all long enough. Let's go!"

Luther was whimpering in pain as Mary C. moved toward the door. Fabian reached down and grabbed the combat knife with his hand and pulled it from its resting place. Luther moaned as the thick blade cut deep again on the way out. Blood gushed out of the gash left behind. Mary C. bent down where Luther was dying.

"I don't think you're gonna come back from the dead this time. You should have helped me, you stupid little boy." She would never tell anyone she had found Luther Rude.

Julius Thurber stepped up to the passenger's side window of Rebecca's truck. It scared her when he opened the door and jumped in. "Get goin'."

"Where's the others?"

"Just go. You want out, don't ya?" Rebecca did want out, and it was time to go.

Jason was standing outside the room when his mother and Fabian came out. His heart jumped as she moved past him. He hated seeing her swollen and bruised face. Jack Jarvis joined the others as they headed for the main house and the truck.

The foursome turned the corner at the side of the house. Rebecca's truck was not there. Fabian was prepared for whatever came their way. "Jason, give me the key to your truck. See if you can start the Corvette, and get Mary C. out of here."

Mary C. held the sheet around her abused body. "I got a spare key taped under the tag." She turned to Jack Jarvis. "I'd kiss you, but I stink too bad. But, you got one comin' whenever you want to collect it. After you win tomorrow, you can buy me dinner."

Jack Jarvis shook his head as Mary C. walked away with Jason. She was too cool. Fabian ran to Jason's truck. He was going to find Rebecca Milkduds Coolie. The red Corvette came sliding around the corner of the house, throwing dirt and dust into the air. Jack Jarvis smiled again when he saw Mary C. was at the wheel. Cool might not be the word for her.

As the Corvette rolled on the one road off of Black Hammock Island, Aunt Annie rolled over in her big bed and put her arm over the bare back of Crew Cut. She had no idea Blondie was not in the bed with them.

With the ferry docked until dawn, Mary C. and Jason had to drive the long way back to Mayport. They would ride through Oceanway, New Berlin, downtown Jacksonville, Arlington and on to Mayport. Fabian took a wild guess and turned toward Fernandina to try and catch up with Rebecca Coolie and have a final showdown with Julius Thurber.

Jack Jarvis was trying to get some greatly needed sleep. He felt good about helping Mary C. and the way she told him to win the fight. He knew he would collect his kiss as soon as possible. He was anxious to see the reaction from Aunt Annie and her associates when they found out about the daring escape that took place during the night.

Fabian slowed the truck down as he rolled off the wooden bridge of the Nassau Sound. He was a few miles from Fernandina. He looked to his right and saw the dust from a moving vehicle moving down a side dirt road. He knew the road was leading to Little Talbot Island. He had fished there before with his father. He knew the truck was moving fast and far enough away that the driver would not know he was being followed.

Rebecca was driving her truck. "I must be crazy. Why would we turn off the main road?"

Julius was nervous but gave her an answer. "We need to lay low for a while. They could be after us. If we stay on that open road, they'll catch us."

"That's crazy. If they've got Mary C., they won't be looking for us. Not yet anyway, but she'll be comin' after me as soon as she can. That's why we need to keep movin'. We can be halfway through Georgia before mornin'. They won't chase me that far. Now, I'm gonna wait in the woods and waste time that we could be movin'."

"Nobody's gonna find us. We'll sit tight for a while and then head out. Just relax. Ol' Quasimodo won't let anything happen to his Esmeralda." Rebecca knew she was making a huge mistake, but she also knew Julius Thurber was crazy about her and just plain crazy. She would bide her time and call him "daddy" again, if need be.

The sun was coming up out of the Atlantic Ocean. Mary C. stood at the bottom step of Mr. King's front porch wrapped in the nasty sheet. Mr. King stood on the porch above her. He was so bewildered by her appearance he was speechless. Mary C. looked up but did not go up the steps. Jason stood behind her.

"John, I need to get in the house and take a long shower. Can we talk about this later?"

Mr. King knew the right answer. "Of course, can I do something to help?"

Mary C. dropped the sheet from her bruised and naked body. It fell to the ground at her feet. Mr. King got a full frontal view of her female attributes. Jason had the rear view.

"You can burn this rag for me. It shouldn't go into the house." Mary C. walked up the steps and into the house. Mr. King tried not to turn as she passed him, but he could not help it; no man could. He watched her walk up the stairs to the upper level of the house. Mary C. walked on her toes causing her bruised butt cheek and calf muscles to flex with every step. Mr. King turned to Jason with his eyes full of questions.

That same sun was starting the day on Black Hammock Island. At least fifty fighting roosters all began to crow as the big orange ball woke them up. All of the full-time fiddler crabs and overnight visitors were wide awake from the irritating sound from the competitive fowl.

Aunt Annie was feeling the aftermath of a night of drinking and sexually abusing other human beings. She had a hangover headache stomping in her big ugly head. She was prepared for the roosters to cause their usual noise and confusion, but it still did not help the pounding in her head. Crew Cut put a pillow over her head to block out the noises. Aunt Annie looked around the room for Blondie, but the tall beauty was gone.

Fabian stopped his truck on the dirt road leading to the Atlantic Ocean. He knew he was close to the beach, and the vehicle he was chasing had stopped at the edge of the sand dunes. He had no idea a beautiful blonde was lying in the back bed of his truck under a blanket. Blondie had found her way out of her bondage on Black

Hammock Island. Her name was Lulu Vesta and she was indebted to Aunt Annie, becoming one of her perverted lovers in order to survive and pay off her debt. Lulu finally realized Aunt Annie was never going to allow her to leave the island. When she heard them talking about the plan to rescue Mary C. and the others and leave the island, she took the opportunity to get away. So far her brave decision had paid off. She lay still as Fabian got out of the truck and began walking toward the beach. He was armed and ready to do battle. He knew he would have to kill Julius Thurber if he was to take Rebecca Coolie back with him to Mayport.

Mary C. scrubbed her battered body inside and out until the hot water was gone. The change in water temperature did not faze her as she continued the deep cleaning. She was raw and chaffed in tender places, but she endured the pain to feel as clean as she could. The cold water bounced off her shoulders as her blood boiled in her veins. She wanted to find Miss Stark's necklace. She wanted Rebecca Coolie back in Mayport. She wanted to kiss Jack Jarvis. She wanted Aunt Annie dead.

CHAPTER FIVE

Aunt Annie stood in the doorway of the small building where Mary C. had been abused and held captive. Crew Cut was kneeling down on the bloody floor next to Luther Rude's dead body. She looked up at Aunt Annie.

"He ain't got a drop of blood left in him. The cut damn near took his head off."

There was fire in Aunt Annie's bloodshot eyes. "I'm scared they might of hurt Lulu. I want the buildings searched right now. Find Julius, wake Rebecca up. I want some answers! There'll be five hundred people on the island in the next few hours. I don't need this shit right now. Find 'em all!"

Two men came into the room as Crew Cut was leaving. Her real name was Ida Gold, and she had spent a year as a member of the Florida female chain gang with Aunt Annie. Aunt Annie protected her when she was in prison, and Ida was completely dedicated to Aunt Annie with no limitations as to what she would do to please her former protector and now lover. The men picked Luther's body up off of the floor and made sure the visitors would not see nor hear anything about his bloody and brutal death.

Mary C. stood in front of the mirror over the dresser in her bedroom. She turned from side to side as she had done many times in her life. The scratches and blood bruises made her think of the abuse she took at the hands of James Thorn. The damage to her body looked similar to that time of pain and anger.

The large expected crowd was gathering on Black Hammock Island. Pickup trucks outnumbered the other vehicles four to one. Confederate flags flew the colors of the region. Aunt Annie was in the main house exploding with anger and rage. Crew Cut and two of the male fiddler crabs were taking the brunt of her tantrum.

"What do you mean 'they're all gone'?"

Ida Gold trembled inside at the reality that she had to be the one who answered the question. "Well...it looks like whoever killed Luther took Mary C., Rebecca and Lulu with 'em. They probably took Lulu as a hostage in case we caught 'em."

The reality of the situation was slapping Aunt Annie in her manly face. "No, that's not true! Lulu ran off on her own. I shoulda seen it comin'. I've been too trustin' lately. I've been too soft. It's time to get mean!" She looked out the front window of the main house as the trucks and cars filled with fight fans came rolling in. "I can't worry 'bout it right now. We're gonna make a fortune today. We ain't never had a fight like this."

Ida Gold took a deep breath, took a chance, and shared her thoughts. "I think the Green Beret Rebecca told us about took out Luther."

Aunt Annie did not like that thought. "When did you become an expert on killers?"

Ida was sorry she had said anything, but it was done. "I'm not, but it just looked like whoever did it sure knew what he was doin'. And to get all those people out of here during the night sure took an organized plan."

Aunt Annie took her own deep breath. "Maybe we should put a few more armed guards in the crowd today to take care of any foolishness."

Aunt Annie always stationed armed personnel in the crowds to stop any disturbance. She doubled the guards and instructed them to be prepared and use their guns if need be. It was four hours before fight time. It would be the largest crowd ever to have assembled on Black Hammock Island.

Officers David Boos and Paul Short were dressed like the locals. They looked like they belonged in Red Neck City. Their heads were on swivels as they walked among the island regulars. With so many new faces and outsiders, no one gave them a second look. It was easy to get lost in such a loud and active crowd. The cock fights were extremely bloody as the winner not only overcame the loser, but the attack with beaks, talons and spurs continued until the victim was a pile of blood-stained feathers. The dog fights were just as cruel and brutal. Angered dog owner and trainers would sometimes beat the losing dog even more after the fight. One time the losing dog was shot during the fight by its owner, because the dog seemed to be quitting. The two officers also saw the aftermath and results of the earlier fights, when they saw dead dogs and roosters being thrown into a deep pit for the victims and losers. Each animal that was injured was put out of its misery and dropped into the deep hole. The Black Hammock clean-up system was quick and thorough. Both officers had guns in ankle holsters just in case they had to defend themselves. They were just observers and had to make a mental note of what they saw and heard.

The two undercover policemen followed a group of men to a building behind the main house. The building was full of shelves and boxes. It was like a huge bargain basement department store, brand names and all. It was organized by the goods presented. One area was for guns, hunting and fishing equipment. Stolen Army surplus goods and gear filled one wall with hundreds of items from boots to roach killing spray bombs. There was even an area with cases of canned goods, cold drinks and beer. The hard whiskey area was the most popular with cases of Jack Daniels, Jim Bean and Wild Turkey sold at rock bottom prices. Black Hammock Island was the ultimate barter town and trading post.

Officer Boos motioned to Officer Short to go out a side door of the building. When they got outside, they found themselves facing a line of six small square buildings. About fifty men were standing and sitting around waiting for their turn to perform their preferred sexual act with one of the working female fiddler crabs of Black Hammock Island.

The officers left the group and went back to the area where the fighting ring was constructed. The ring was elevated on wooden posts with a twenty square feet plywood floor. The sides of the ring were roped off, but there was also an eight foot high section of chicken wire enclosing the square. The fight fans were drinking, eating and jockeying for the best positions to watch the battle.

Fabian Moore moved through the oak trees, cabbage palms and sand dunes without a sound or any disturbance at all. He was a quiet killing machine. Even with the evil living in Julius Thurber's black heart, the serial killer did not hold a candle to the force driving Fabian Moore. He loved the anticipation, and he loved the hunt itself. He heard voices on the other side of the dune. It was Rebecca Coolie.

"I can't believe we left the road like this. Stop touching me. We've gotta plan this thing out, and all you want is for me to spread my legs right here in the sand. They're gonna come lookin' for us."

"They ain't gonna find us. I just thought we could enjoy each other 'til it was safe to move on."

"Stop it, I said. Just let's get out of here."

"We gonna do it one time, and then we'll go. That's the way it is."

Rebecca was quiet after his statement and tone. She knew being alone on the isolated beach gave her no choice. Julius started to undress her. Her top was first, so he could look at her breasts. He sucked on one of her big nipples and moved his hand down inside her shorts. Julius Thurber's black heart raced in his chest when he saw a pair of black army boots in the sand next to him.

Fabian Moore did not care that Julius Thurber had saved Jason's life at another time and place. He knew the first time he saw Julius that he would have to kill him eventually. It was just understood. Fabian knew he could not hesitate or give any quarter to a man like Julius Thurber. The combat knife cut deep and true with the first swing of Fabian's strong and accurate arm. Again, it was the perfect throat cut. Julius Thurber was dead when his face hit the soft white sand of Little Talbot Island.

Rebecca Coolie screamed and jumped to her feet. She was still topless with her huge breasts pointing at Fabian. He could see the pure fear in her young eyes. The soft beach sand was already absorbing the heavy flow of blood from the cut on the big man's throat. Rebecca's legs trembled when she saw Fabian staring into her eyes.

"Please don't kill me. I didn't mean for all this to happen. I was scared of everybody. Please don't kill me. I'll give the necklace back; just don't kill me. I'm eighteen years old. I don't want to die here on the beach next to him." She looked down at Julius Thurber then back into Fabian's eyes.

Fabian wiped the blade of the knife on his pants. "I can't kill you, Rebecca. I'm crazy about ya."

Mary C. walked out onto Mr. King's front porch. Once again, she was dressed to kill, but this time it was not to attract men; it was actually to kill. Jason was opening the driver's side door of the Corvette.

"Where you goin'?"

Jason turned to see his mother dressed to hide her body. The hat and sunglasses she wore were to hide her face. Jason had never seen his mother in such attire. "I was goin' to get Billy. Sofia and Margie took him last night, so I could go get Fabian."

"Give me the keys."

Jason handed her the keys to the Corvette. Mary C. walked to the back of the car and opened up the trunk. She took out her weapon of choice. Jason waited for his mother to tell him what to do next. Mary C. checked the gun to be sure it was loaded. Mr. King walked out of the house. He was also surprised at the unusual way Mary C. was dressed. He listened to Mary C. as she talked to Jason.

"I'm goin' back out there." She turned to Mr. King. "John, I need the keys to your car." Mr. King reached into his pants pocket, pulled out his car keys, and tossed them to Mary C. She caught the keys with her free hand while holding the shotgun in her other hand.

"I'll go with ya, Mama."

Mary C. moved to the driver's side door of Mr. King's 1957 Chevy. "I wanted you to go, but, on second thought, I'll be better alone. I'll just have to worry about me. I won't make the same mistakes I made last time." She looked up at Mr. King. "I heard Anna Jo Hamilton's still alive and flyin' in the area. All this time we thought she was dead. It was strange thinkin' 'bout her. It probably ain't true. I ain't sure how I felt about it."

"Who told you Anna Jo was alive?"

"We'll talk about it when I get back. You can think about her while I'm gone. Maybe it will take your mind off of Norman."

Mr. King's eye lit up. "Now don't make fun of Norman. He got my doily back, didn't he?"

Mary C. could not respond to Mr. King's praise of a ghost finding and returning the white doily from the chair, but she had another thought she had to share. "I'll bet you a bar-b-que dinner at the Red Barn that you think about Anna Jo for the rest of the day and into the night. I'll trust your word as a boat captain and Mayport gentleman that you'll tell me the truth when I get back. Hell, John, I thought you and Anna Jo was gonna get together for a while there. Mayport's haunted house man and the first witch to live here havin' their little goblins runnin' around the docks castin' spells and talkin' to the dead. We were all pretty relieved when that union never took place." Even with the danger facing Mary C. at Black Hammock Island, she still had her strange sense of humor. "We'll talk about what I heard when I get back."

Mr. King knew it was useless to try and stop Mary C. from her mission. He would think about Anna Jo Hamilton. It was exciting for him to have Anna Jo around when she was trying to teach others about the Wicca way. She was the first real witch he knew of to set up residence in Mayport. It was all fascinating to him and it fit in with his haunted house.

Mr. King had very little contact with Anna Jo at first, but she did become a regular visitor to his haunted house so she could feel the presence of the other side. He was attracted to Anna Jo, but at first he was afraid if she was a real witch and he was too forward, she may not like it and turn him into a horny toad. His fears were lifted when Anna Jo, the witch, was also Anna Jo, the woman of the flesh and physical desires. Hoping to reach the underworld by being in Mr. King's house, Anna Jo used her beauty and her witchcraft to drive John King crazy with passion and sexual wants.

Lulu Vesta was still hiding under the blanket in the back of the truck when she heard the sound of another truck engine. Rebecca was driving and Fabian was sitting in the passenger's seat. The truck stopped and Fabian got out and into the other truck. He followed Rebecca back toward the main road. No one was there to see them, but the buzzards were already landing in the trees near Julius Thurber's body.

Mary C. drove Mr. King's 1957 Chevy off of the ferry on the Ft. George side of the St. Johns River. She looked to her left and then her right to be sure the coast was clear so she could turn left toward Oceanway. She saw two trucks coming toward her. She recognized Jason's truck then realized the other truck belonged to Rebecca Coolie. She knew Fabian would not recognize Mr. King's car, so she blew the horn and drove back into the parking area at the ferry slip. Both trucks slowed down and drove into the parking lot. Mary C. jumped out of the car so Fabian could see her. He was not sure who it was at first until Mary C. took her hat off. He jumped out of the truck and ran to her.

"You alright? What are you doin' here?"

Mary C. looked at Rebecca Coolie sitting in her truck. She could see the fear and hate in the young girl's eyes. Mary C. talked to Fabian but continued her stare with the Coolie girl. "I do love you, Fabian Moore."

He smiled, but was still concerned. "What are you doin' here like this? Where's Jason?"

"He's home. I'm goin' back out there. There ain't no other way for me. You take Miss Coolie back, and we'll all have a long talk tonight. I'm goin' to see a man give another man a real old-fashioned ass whippin'. Then I'm gonna repay Aunt Annie for her true southern hospitality." Mary C. walked to Rebecca Coolie and stood at the truck window. "I'm tired of this. You stay put, and we'll make a deal when I get back."

Rebecca did not respond with words, but her eyes said, "Yes, ma'am."

Jack Jarvis was still sitting in his room. He would not go outside until it was time to fight. His mammoth opponent Virgil Grave Digger Hartley was eating pancakes, bacon and eggs and washing it all down with a Schlitz Beer. Aunt Annie and Crew Cut were walking among the visitors making sure everyone was enjoying themselves and getting whatever they needed. Aunt Annie was quite the despicable hostess.

Fabian watched the 1957 Chevy roll away and onto the main road toward Oceanway and Black Hammock Island. The ferry horn blew announcing the big carrier was leaving the Mayport side and was only a few minutes away. Lulu Vesta was hot and uncomfortable under the blanket in the back of the truck, but she dare not show herself. She had no idea how they would react to her being there, but she had a strong feeling it would not be very pleasant. She thought the man might even kill her.

There was one hour before fight time. The crowd was loud and full of food and drink. Aunt Annie had an area to place bets on a favorite fighter with her getting a percentage of each and every bet, win or lose. Officers Boos and Short were standing near the chicken wire ring when Aunt Annie walked past them.

"You boys ready for a hell of a fight?" The question surprised both policemen, but Paul Short smiled and shook his head. Aunt Annie smiled back. "Drink up, boys, and don't forget you gotta make your bets before the fight starts. Oh yeah, and after the fight we got women to ease your pain if ya lose." Some of the crowd laughed, and some moaned at her heartless sense of humor. She laughed and moved on with Ida Crew Cut Gold trailing behind her.

The ferry was pulling into the slip on the Ft. George side. Fabian was standing at the driver's side window of Rebecca's truck. She was scared. "What do you think she'll do to me?"

He was quick with his answer. "Nothin' if you give her the necklace. I'm not gonna let her hurt ya, but you gotta give it to her."

"She said we can make a deal, but I don't trust her."

"If she said that, then she'll do it. Just please don't get scared and run again."

She smiled at Fabian. She knew she had him in the palm of her hand or, better yet, between her legs. The ferry was docking. Fabian took a deep breath.

"I could have left you bleedin' on the beach with your new boyfriend, but you're here safe with me. You do know that, don't ya?" Her throat went dry, and she was scared again. She nodded, but had no words. "If you run again, you won't have to worry about Mary C., because I'll be the one hunting you down. I hope you understand what I'm sayin'." She nodded her pretty head again. "Good. Now, get on the ferry, and go to my house. Theda will be happy to see you. Don't make a fool of me this time. We'll both meet with Mary C. tonight and get this thing over with once and for all. Remember, I am absolutely crazy about you, but you can't snake me again. A man can forgive a woman just so many times." He put his hand in his pocket and handed her a dollar to pay for the ferry ride back to Mayport.

Mary C. drove up to the main gate to the road leading to Black Hammock Island. The gate was open, but an armed guard was standing in the middle of the opening. She stopped the Chevy as he approached the window. He had to look into the car to see if the driver was a man or a woman. "What's your business here, ma'am?"

"My business? I guess it's like everybody else's business. I'm here to see the fight."

"And what fight is that, ma'am?"

"What is this, a test or somethin'?"

"You might say that."

"The fight is between Jack Jarvis and Grave Digger. And I can't wait to tell Aunt Annie you stopped me from bringin' her supply of Slim Jims to the house. She also called me her 'new main squeeze' last night when she had her tongue up my ass. So you go ahead and keep askin' me these stupid questions, and I'll mention what an asshole you are when I'm feedin' her these Slim Jims." Mary C. pointed to a case of Slim Jims sitting on the seat next to her. She had stopped and bought them just in case she needed an excuse to enter the island.

"I'm just doin' my job, ma'am. Please don't take it personal. Ain't no reason to tell Aunt Annie nothin'. If I offended you, that wasn't my intention." A truck rolled up behind the Chevy as the man was apologizing. "Move on now, ma'am. Enjoy the fight."

Fabian made sure Rebecca drove her truck onto the ferry before he left. He knew he was taking a huge gamble that she would do as he told her, but he could not allow Mary C. to face Black Hammock Island alone. It was his specialty, and he wanted to feel the rush of the battle as much as he wanted to feel the rush of Rebecca Coolie. When the ferry horn sounded to make the crossing back to Mayport, Fabian drove the truck out onto the main road and turned toward Black Hammock Island.

Jason walked up onto Miss Margaret's front porch and knocked on the door. Sofia opened the door with a beautiful smile and greeting. "Hey, Jason, come on in." She looked at the red Corvette. "Oh, wow, you're driving the new car." Jason followed her into the house where they were greeted by Miss Margaret. She was holding Billy in her arms.

"Well, hey, Daddy. I was hoping you wouldn't come for Billy until later. It is so much fun having a baby in the house again. If you have things to do today, I'd love to keep him a little longer. The girls will be in and out today from the store, so I'll have him to myself most of the day. I really haven't had very much time with him until this morning." She smiled at her long winded request. "Listen to me babbling on like this. If it's okay, I'd like to babysit him today, and when you come back to get him this evening, I'd like you to stay for dinner. Tell Mary C. and John to come, too."

Sofia's ice-blue eyes lit up at her mother's idea. She was trying to find her old feelings for Jason, and having him around was a good start. She tried not to act excited, but she was. "Yes, Jason, come have supper with us. I'll make some banana pudding."

Jason smiled and spoke for the first time since he had arrived. "That'll be good. I'd like that." He turned to Miss Margaret. "You sure you don't mind?"

"I'm the one asking you. Of course I don't mind. We'll see you for supper." She moved toward Jason with Billy, so he could kiss his son good-by. Jason kissed Billy on the cheek and turned to leave. Sofia did not want him to go.

"Have you had any breakfast, yet?"

Miss Margaret smiled. "It's eleven-thirty, Sofia. It's almost lunch time."

"Well, have you had lunch, yet? Miss Margaret smiled again and left them in the living room. She still did not like the hold Jason had on her youngest daughter. Sofia had changed considerably since Jason entered her young life. Miss Margaret did not want Sofia to be with him.

Jason stepped out onto the front porch as Sofia followed him. "I'll come for supper, but I need to go now. I need to help Mama with a few things and then get the boat ready. Thanks for keeping Billy." He walked to the Corvette and left Sofia standing on the porch.

Mary C. stopped the car next to another man who was collecting ten dollars a person to enter the island and see the fight. She had to park about a hundred yards away from the chicken wire square. That was perfect for her to get lost in the crowd of late comers as they walked to the ring.

The fight was only ten minutes away. Grave Digger was in the ring stirring the emotions of the spectators into a pre-fight frenzy. Some were cheering; some were jeering. It was a split crowd as to which man was the favorite. Some of the crowd laughed out loud at Grave Digger's fighting attire.

Virgil Hartley needed his mother there to dress him properly. He wore black, skin tight, stretch pants that left nothing to the imagination as to the size of his penis and ball sack. He could have easily had two live squirrels trapped in the front of his pants. He still wore the black Converse All-Star tennis shoes on his feet. Grave Digger's muscle shirt was bright orange and looked like he had taken it from an old time circus strong man from the 1800's. The Halloween colors were perfect for his ridiculous costume.

Jack Jarvis walked out of the main house and onto the front porch. He looked toward the noisy crowd and could see his black and orange Neanderthal opponent standing tall in the middle of the ring. Jack had to shake his head and smile at the vision. He knew Virgil Grave Digger Hartley would be the biggest individual he had faced up to that point of his fighting career.

Aunt Annie was also standing in the ring. She was in a corner and would soon welcome the paying spectators and introduce the two combatants. Ida Gold was standing on the outside of the ring next to Aunt Annie. Aunt Annie was worried about Jack Jarvis waiting until the last minute to come to the ring, if he was coming at all. She whispered to Crew Cut. "Go see where he is. Nobody's seen him since last night. I hope he ain't run off, too."

Ida looked toward the main house. "He's walkin' this way now."

Aunt Annie motioned to one of her fiddler crabs to turn on the music she had picked for the introduction of the fight. Two large cone shaped speakers suspended from a tree blasted out Aunt Annie's theme song for the day. The crowd went crazy again as they saw the Jackal approaching the ring and the music blasted out over their heads. The song from the western movie "High Noon" sent the crowd beyond frenzy. Frankie Lane's distinctive voice filled the pre-fight air.

Do not forsake me, oh, my darling, on this our wedding day-ay.

The cheers and laughter from the spectators continued as Jack Jarvis worked his way to the ring. They loved the fact one of the stars of the day was walking among them. Jack Jarvis knew how to win the crowd.

The music continued to blast out over their heads. Officer Paul Short turned to his partner David Boos. "I think we've seen enough to bring in the troops, don't you?"

David Boos understood. "I think so. You wanna watch the fight, and then we'll get out of here?" They both smiled and joined the fight crowd.

Jack Jarvis was slowly making his way through his admiring fans. People love touching and being near the celebrities. Grave Digger was yelling and pointing at Jack, but the music and crowd noise covered his taunting words.

Mary C. had moved to the middle of the crowd as Jack walked past her. He did not recognize her at all. She had to smile when she saw that he was carrying a full bottle of Jack Daniels whiskey in his hand. She understood why he would do such a thing before the fight. Mary C. remembered the night her man Hawk drank Jack Daniels before his historic fight with Big Zeke Shackelford at Bill's Hideaway. Big Zeke also drank his share of the "nectar of the working man" before the fight. Mary C. knew the hard liquor would numb some of the pain the fighters would endure when engaging in a pugilistic situation.

Chills ran down Mary C.'s spine when Jack stepped up on the edge of the ring and turned the open bottle of Jack Daniels up to his lips. The crowd cheered in anticipation of what was to come. He held the bottle up as he drank a quarter of the liquid in one gulp. He stepped up to the ring entrance but stopped before he entered. Jack turned to the crowd and took another long swallow of the gold nectar. The noise of the crowd was deafening. Aunt Annie loved it as she waited in the ring.

Mary C.'s heart raced again, and she was caught up in the frenzy. She looked at Aunt Annie in order to get her mind back to the task at hand. She felt that her previous relationship with Jack Jarvis was the reason Aunt Annie was able to foil her earlier attempt to take Rebecca away. Mary C. could not allow him to take her attention. Jack had one more antic to ignite the crowd and win more of their support.

He handed the half empty bottle of Jack Daniels to a pretty young woman who was standing near him at ringside. She turned the bottle up to her mouth and took a drink. When she moved the bottle away from her lips Jack reached down with his powerful hands, picked her up, and kissed her with the moisture from the liquor still on both their lips. The crowd went absolutely wild. It was the loudest explosion of noise ever to pierce the air surrounding Black Hammock Island. It was going to be a day to remember for all who were there. It was a day for making legends. It was a day for killing.

Mary C.'s heart danced as Jack Jarvis gently put the young woman down. He was that breed of man who could move the masses of both men and women. Jack Jackal Jarvis was definitely

Mary C.'s kind of man. He stepped through the opening in the chicken wire, to the loud approval of the crowd and finally stood in the ring facing his opponent. Jack Jarvis was barefoot. He wore blue sweat pants and a white t-shirt. Jack bounced on his toes from one side of the ring to the other and never took his eyes off of Grave Digger.

Aunt Annie held up her hands to get the attention of the frenzied crowd and quiet them down. Frankie Lane's voice blasting out over the speakers went silent and the fifth playing of the song *High Noon* ended. The crowd got quiet so Aunt Annie could make the introductions. She walked to the middle of the ring.

"Ladies and Gentlemen, welcome to the Fight Week main event on Black Hammock Island!" The crowd erupted again. They were looking for any reason to whoop and holler, but Aunt Annie loved it all. She had practiced her speech for a week, and she could hardy wait to present it. The onlookers calmed as she made the introductions.

"In the far corner, to my right, stands a giant of a man. Well over three hundred pounds and standing six foot, nine inches." Aunt Annie looked directly at Grave Digger's bulge in the front of his pants. "And I think I see where another nine inches might be hidin'." The crowd roared with laughter at her suggestive joke. Grave Digger grabbed himself and grinned like a growling opossum. Aunt Annie waited for the crowd to calm down, so she could continue her introduction. "When he ain't crackin' skulls, he makes his home in Palm Valley, Florida as a member of the famous fighting Hartley family. He has never been knocked off his feet and has never tasted defeat in twenty-six fights. Ladies, gentlemen, and fiddler crabs, his mama calls him Virgil, but she ain't here, so we call him… 'Grave Digger'!"

The crowd went wild as she pointed to Grave Digger and he jumped to the middle of the ring to bathe in the praise and admiration. Most of the women in the audience were happy he did not try to kiss them as Jack Jarvis had done. He was one ugly man. Actually, he was so big he looked like two ugly men. He stepped back to his corner as Aunt Annie began talking again. The crowd calmed somewhat as she continued.

"In the corner to my left is the second warrior of our main event. He stands six foot, three inches tall and weighs two-hundred thirty pounds. He is unbeaten in twenty-two fights and has never been on the floor. He's been called 'Triple J', his mama calls him Jack, but today he's the Jackal. Ladies and gentlemen, I give you a favorite with both man and woman, Jack, the Jackal, Jarvis!"

The crowd was wild again. He had won some new fans but mostly female. That was a good thing, because the women yelled and cheered the loudest.

Aunt Annie held her hands in the air to silence the crowd. She had been waiting to throw her favorite saying to the spectators. It was her trademark when it was time for the Fight Week main event. The regulars in the crowd would chant it along with her, and the newcomers would remember to say it the next time. The crowd was quiet enough for her to be heard. Aunt Annie stood between the two Black Hammock gladiators and yelled as loud as she could. "Remember, gentlemen, you can't break no rules." She stopped and allowed the crowd to finish her statement…"cause there ain't no rules!" Aunt Annie loved it when that happened.

She left the ring through the chicken wire gate to stand with Ida Gold. "You hear that? I love it when they repeat, 'there ain't no rules'." Ida smiled. If Aunt Annie was happy, Ida Gold was happy.

One of the fiddler crabs closed the gate, and the fighters were left alone in the ring. There would be no referee, no one to stop the fight if one of the combatants became disabled to the point of not being able to continue or defend himself. It was up to the other fighter to determine when it was time to end the brutal beating.

Jack Jarvis had beaten all comers so far, and he never had to kill anyone. Grave Digger got his name from the fact that four of his twenty-six fights had ended in the death of his opponent. His crushing blow to a man's head could be fatal. Jack Jarvis said he fought for the money, but he knew in reality he absolutely adored every second of the fight. When he knew he had a man beaten, Jack would not continue the attack. No opponent had ever challenged him for a re-match.

Fabian Moore stopped the truck at the gate to Black Hammock Island as an armed guard held his hand up. He stepped to the driver's side window. "State ya business, mister."

Fabian had the answer. "I'm here for the fight. I stayed here last night but had to leave to take care of some business, and I been hurrying so I wouldn't be late. And wouldn't ya know it, I'm late anyway."

The guard looked at his watch. "Fight just started right now, high noon. Can't let nobody in after it starts. Aunt Annie's orders. You can come in after but not now."

Fabian was hoping to solve the problem at hand peacefully. "I even bunked in last night with Mr. Jarvis. I told him I'd cheer for him from the crowd."

The guard shook his head. "You shoulda stayed inside, mister. I'm sorry."

Fabian nodded. "I'm sorry, too." He put the truck gear in reverse and started backing up the truck. The guard turned away and faced the wooden gate for a second. He heard the truck engine roar, but it was too late when he turned around. The low front bumper hit him right above his knees, breaking his femur bone in both legs. The terrified man heard his leg bones crack first, then the wood from the gate shattered as the front of the truck blasted the guard into the closed gate. Pieces of the wood splintered and stuck into his back and butt cheeks. He was not dead when the impact of the truck threw his body into the muddy ditch next to the road, but he would not follow the intruder or tell Aunt Annie he was on his way. His eyes were blurred by shock and pain, so he only heard the truck drive away toward Black Hammock Island.

Jason stopped the Corvette in front of Fabian Moore's house. He had a burning desire to see Theda. He saw her looking out the front window. She ran to the front door when she realized Jason had retuned.

Fabian Moore entered the crowd as the two fighters moved toward each other. He was looking for Mary C. The noise from the spectators was again deafening, and the two men had not even thrown one punch or kick. Grave Digger was the first to attack with a big right fist coming down from above. Jack blocked the first punch with his forearm, but he could feel the brute power in Virgil Hartley. Jack decided to be defensive at first and see what Grave Digger had to offer. He knew the crowd would not like his defensive style, but he did not care. They were not the one fighting the monster. Jack bounced up and down on his toes as he had done during his warm up. He did throw a lightning quick left jab that landed on the bridge of Grave Digger's nose and popped his head back in a whiplash movement. The crowd roared as Virgil stopped and absorbed the jab.

Virgil's next strong-arm swing connected high on Jack's shoulder as he moved away. It was a struggle for Jack to keep his feet. He fell into the side chicken wire and was able to catch his balance. The crowd cheered as Grave Digger pinned Jack to the chicken wire and landed three hard licks, two on his upper arms and one on his left ear. The crowd didn't like it when Jack moved away from the chicken wire and did not trade punches with Virgil. Jack knew he had to stay away from Virgil Hartley's destructive right hand. He did not think he could survive a direct blow to his head. The huge man was much quicker with his hands than Jack expected. He knew Grave Digger was going to be a difficult man to beat, but it was too late to run. He had to fight.

Jack Jarvis had perfected what was known as the "spinning back fist." It was his best and favorite maneuver to turn a fight in his favor. He would rotate in a full circle spin motion, creating fast momentum as he would direct the back of his clinched fist toward a target, hopefully, on the face of the opponent. It was even more effective if the target was moving toward the flying fist. It was a gamble, because if he missed, he would be vulnerable for a counter attack. Jack was yet to initiate any offensive attack. The crowd knew it, too, and they were not going to be patient very much longer. Virgil had been the aggressor up to that point. Jack knew he would not be able to grapple with Virgil if they were to fall to the floor of the ring. If Grave Digger got his huge strong hands on Jack, he knew he would not be able to win the fight. Jack had to stay on his feet. Virgil surprised Jack when he made a wild bull-like charge across the ring. The wild maneuver prompted Jack to take the chance and attempt the "spinning back fist."

The speed of Jack's spin was lightning fast causing the momentum to deliver the full impact possible. The back of Jack's hand hit Virgil on the corner of his left eye near the temple. The connection sounded like a cannon going off. The spectators made a single noise of shock and awe when the sound of the lick actually seemed to echo off the trees and then linger in the air. A one-inch wide, horse-shoe cut opened up a half circle gash around Virgil's eye. Grave Digger had never taken such a devastating blow during his exceedingly successful fighting career. The crowd gasped as the monster man took a number of staggering steps backward to get his balance and to survey what just actually happened.

Jack knew from the feel of the connection he had hurt Virgil. How much damage occurred was yet to be determined. He was pleased with how it felt. Jack looked down at the front bulge in Virgil's tight pants. He wanted to kick that sack of squirrels right out of the ring. He knew that would end the fight. He also knew if Grave Digger had the same opportunity he would pull Jack's genitals off of his body and hand them as a Fight Week souvenir to the young woman Jack had kissed before the fight. Jack Jarvis could not bring himself to kick another man in his privates. It just was not his way.

CHAPTER SIX

Jason was in Theda's bed with the fifteen-year-old sitting across him. Once again he was deep inside her, and the combination of sexual pain and pleasure caused her to scream with pure delight. Each time she would calm down, Jason would push up and pound her again, causing the same audible reaction. It was interesting that even with his mother in possible grave danger, Jason had the mindset to pleasure himself with his new sex partner.

Dark blood gushed from the deep cut over Grave Digger's left eye. He pawed at the eye with the back of his hand in an attempt to wipe away the blood and get some of his vision back. The crowd screamed for Jack to continue his attack. Jack Jarvis knew he could not give his dangerous and formidable opponent any measure of time to recover. He had never waited before and would not start now. There was no thought of mercy at all. Virgil did not see the next punch when Jack threw it. It was a straight right hand that drove his knuckles into Grave Digger's rib cage directly under the monster's heart. Jack was aware of the damage such a blow to the heart could do to a man. All the air exploded out of Virgil's full lungs. He literally had his breath knocked out of his body and out of the chicken wire ring.

Jack made a third attack using the outside of his hand in a chopping motion to Virgil's throat and protruding Adam's apple. Grave Digger thought his apple had been driven to the back of his neck, or perhaps he had swallowed it. Having the breath knocked out of him had now become the least of Virgil Hartley's worries.

Jack's final attack was a direct kick to the outside of Virgil's right knee. When his leg broke, it could no longer hold the weight of the rest of his body. He crumbled like a sugar cookie to the plywood floor of the ring. The excited and stunned crowd drowned out the noises of agony coming from Virgil Hartley's throat. The fight was not quite three minutes old and it was over. Jack's longest fight had been a little over six minutes. His appearance and gentlemanly ways did not paint the true picture of Jack Jarvis. He loved it when he surprised his opponents and the spectators. He could hear it in their voices and see it in their faces.

Aunt Annie and some of her male fiddler crabs entered the ring to attend to Virgil Hartley. Jack Jarvis watched as they tried to help the fallen fighter. The crowd noise died down as they looked at Grave Digger and then at Jack. Every man wanted to be like him. Every woman just wanted him. Virgil looked through one good eye at Jack Jarvis as to say, *Who and what the hell are you?*

There was an eerie atmosphere as the crowd went almost completely silent. They were wondering, like Virgil, where such a man came from. It would be an event none who were present would ever forget. Jack was leaving the ring when Aunt Annie gave him a big, sagging-breasted hug. The silence ended when the song "Shot Gun" by Junior Walker and the All Stars blasted out of the speakers.

Mary C. turned her head toward the sound. It was the perfect omen for her to go back to the car and get her weapon of choice. She wanted to put her arms around Jack Jarvis, but she wanted to kill Aunt Annie first.

Lulu Vesta lifted the blanket off of her head and pushed her body up from the back bed of the truck. She looked over the side railing. Her heart screamed when she realized she had come full circle and had returned to Black Hammock Island. She did not see one of Aunt Annie's fiddler crabs walk up to the truck.

"Hey, Lulu, you alright? Some fight, huh?"

Lulu was surprised but was able to keep her wits about her. "I'm fine, Harry. Yes, it was a great fight. I know Aunt Annie was pleased with the turn out."

"What ya doin' in this truck? You need some help?"

"I was lookin' into the window. I think the owner of this truck had somethin' to do with all that trouble here last night. We need to tell Aunt Annie he might be back to do something else."

"Come on, I'll help ya down." Lulu allowed Harry to help her get out of the truck bed, and he became her unwanted escort to Aunt Annie.

Food, liquor, music, dancing, cards and women were on the Saturday post-fight agenda on Black Hammock Island. Once the fight was over, the crowd moved on to their individual interests. Aunt Annie had instructed some of her fiddler crabs to put Grave Digger in the back of a truck and drive him to St. Luke's Hospital in Jacksonville. They were moving fast but stopped at the broken main gate. The driver knew something was wrong. He got out of the truck and looked at the shattered gate. He turned to the two other fiddler crabs who were sitting in the back of the truck giving what comfort they could to the injured Virgil Hartley.

"Ain't sure what we got here, boys. Who was on the gate?" Both men shook their heads and shrugged their shoulders. They did not know. It was too strange for the driver to let it go. He walked to the other side of the truck and saw the injured guard in the ditch.

The driver realized how severe the guard's injuries were when he pulled his broken body up out of the muddy ditch. They placed him in the back of the truck next to Virgil Hartley. The driver turned to one of the fiddler crabs.

"Go on back to the island. Tell Aunt Annie what we found here. I'll get these two poor devils to the hospital."

The party after the fight was in full swing in the main house. Drink and food were not free, but they were sold at discount prices. Jack Jarvis was the center of attention from both the men and women. They wanted to take pictures with him, get his autograph, touch him, and just stand close to him. He could have taken any woman in the room upstairs and had sexual relations. Aunt Annie and Ida Gold stood with him. Aunt Annie was beaming.

"You have created a memorable day here on my island, Mr. Jarvis. You're welcome to fight here any time. That is, if we can find someone to fight ya."

Jack understood the fight game. "You don't have to worry about that, ma'am. There's always somebody who wants to fight. And there's always somebody better."

Aunt Annie held up her glass of Jim Beam and saluted Mr. Jack Jarvis. "Not today, sport, not today."

Jack nodded after her compliment and turned away to sign his name on the bare butt cheek of the pretty young woman he had kissed before the fight. She just dropped her shorts and panties so he would have a big smooth surface to write on. It was a great day on Black Hammock Island with much more excitement to come.

With Theda's bedroom at the back of the house, her wild banshee screams and Jason being lost in the sex, they did not hear Rebecca Coolie knocking on the front door. She was too afraid of Fabian's threat and combat knife that she had decided to take her chances with Mary C. and do what Fabian said and wait for him at the house. She was tired and scared and did need a place to gather her thoughts and get some sleep. Rebecca turned the door knob, and the door was unlocked. She walked in.

"Theda, you here? Theda, it's me, Rebecca." It added to her fear at first when she heard noises coming from down the long hallway. She knew it was Theda. She was going to run, but she listened again and realized Theda was in no trouble. Rebecca knew the sounds of sex and pleasure when she heard them. She slowly moved down the hall and stopped at Theda's bed room door. The door was open a little, and Rebecca looked in to see who or what was taking Theda to such a high level of ecstasy. The vision of Theda in her bed kneeling on all fours and Jason kneeling down behind her caused Rebecca's hot blood to run wild in her veins. She felt heat and moisture between her legs instantly.

Her big nipples hardened and stood out against her shirt. The pumping action of Jason's muscular buttocks added to the forming moisture. Theda let loose with one of her patent banshee screams as Rebecca Coolie lost control of herself and entered the room.

Theda was mentally in another dimension, but Jason felt Rebecca's presence in the room when she approached the bed. He turned his head but continued pumping Theda. Jason smiled and pumped Theda even harder. Rebecca rubbed herself between her legs as she watched. She wasn't sure why, but she was mesmerized by Theda and Jason. Jason smiled again. Rebecca took off her shirt and dropped it to the floor exposing her incredible bare breasts. Jason had heard about her breasts but had never seen them bare and within his reach. He pumped Theda harder to her and Rebecca's delight when Rebecca's breasts seem to point directly at him. Rebecca's nipples were so hard she was afraid they might explode at any second. Jason knew he had never seen the like of Rebecca's breasts. He thought that perhaps Older Peggy's breasts were as big but not as young and firm as Milkduds Coolie's.

Her pants hit the floor, and she stood there so Jason could see her incredible frontal physical attributes. Her body was absolutely beautiful and as close to perfect as it could get. She was a natural beauty. Jason gave Theda two quick deep forward thrusts causing her to scream louder. Rebecca could feel him inside her, too. Theda looked to her left and finally saw Rebecca standing completely nude next to the bed. Jason stopped pumping to give Theda a moment to see their new visitor. Theda dropped her head down on the pillow.

"What's goin' on?"

Rebecca looked at Jason and then back at Theda. "Fabian told me to come here with you until he comes back. I knocked on the door, but I guess you didn't hear me."

Theda looked at Jason. He smiled. She smiled back. He was still kneeling on the bed but had pulled away from his sexual connection to Theda. His manhood was visible for Rebecca to see. Theda had to ask.

"You come here naked?"

Rebecca smiled, too. "No, I didn't. I took off my clothes when I saw you two in here. I can't explain it, but it was the most exciting thing I've ever seen. I never really watched a man and a woman like this before." The sight of Aunt Annie and her two lovers flashed in Rebecca's mind. "My heart's still poundin'."

Jason was still hard and his heart was racing, too. "Y'all stop talkin' and let's finish this." He looked at Rebecca. "You watchin' or joinin' in?"

Rebecca looked at Theda. "It's up to you, Theda."

Theda hesitated for a moment, but Jason's smile and nod of approval answered the question for her. She nodded to Rebecca.

Rebecca Milkduds Coolie crawled into the bed with Jason and Theda.

Mary C. walked toward Mr. King's 1957 Chevy. She had no idea how she would be able to move around carrying her shotgun. She thought of other ways to end Aunt Annie's evil hold and reign on Black Hammock Island. Mary C.'s visit to the island was strictly business at first. She wanted the necklace back. That would have been the end of it. The abuse caused by Aunt Annie had made it all personal now, and there was no turning back.

Aunt Annie's eyes lit up when Lulu Vesta walked into the dining room of the main house. She turned to Ida Gold. "I told you she didn't run away." Ida looked at Aunt Annie as to say, *You did not. You said she did run away*, but that was just a thought.

Aunt Annie moved quickly to her long lost lover. She gave Lulu one of her best sagging breast hugs. Lulu returned the embrace as she looked into the skeptical eyes of Ida Crew Cut Gold. Aunt Annie held Lulu at arms' length. "I knew you didn't run away; I just knew it. Are you okay? What happened?"

Lulu Vesta was ready. "A man came to help Mary C. get away. I think he killed Luther, but I ain't sure."

Aunt Annie interrupted. "Well, somebody did that's for sure, 'cause the poor bastard's dead."

Lulu continued. "They covered me with a blanket and tied me up. I don't know why; they just did. I was in the back of a truck. We dove all over the place."

Aunt Annie had to interrupt again. "Was Rebecca with 'em of her own free will?" Lulu hesitated with her answer. "Well, was Rebecca with 'em or not?"

Lulu hung her head. "Yes, ma'am, she was." Aunt Annie's face was red with anger. Lulu had more information to keep Aunt Annie's mind occupied. "I think the man who killed Luther is here today. I saw his truck. I'm sure he's here."

Aunt Annie raised her voice. "You mean here on the island right now?"

"Yes ma'am, I'm sure of it. And he's a bad man."

Ida Gold stepped to Lulu. "And just how did you manage the get free from this 'bad man,' being tied up and all?"

Lulu Vesta was ready for Ida Gold. "I think when he decided to come back here he knew he couldn't keep me in the truck. I was under a damn blanket."

Aunt Annie interrupted again. "You poor darlin', what you have gone through."

Ida Gold rolled her eyes as she asked her question again. "So, how did you get away?"

"He left me in the woods a few miles up the road. I was still tied up. I guess he was gonna come back and get me later."

Aunt Annie was concerned. "Did they do shit to ya?"

"No, ma'am, but I think he was plannin' too. I was able to get the ropes untied, and here I am."

Ida Gold had heard enough. "I tell ya one thing. You look pretty damn good for someone who's been tied up all night in the back of a truck, was left in the woods, and just walked a few miles to the island. You ain't got no rope bruises on your arms."

Lulu knew she needed to change the direction of the cross examination. She looked at Aunt Annie. "He killed Julius, too. I didn't see it, but I know he did."

Aunt Annie's eyes lit up. "Julius left with y'all?"

"No, ma'am, he was tryin' to save us and make Rebecca come back. The man killed him and took Rebecca to the Mayport ferry. She went across, and he came back here.

Ida Gold knew Lulu was lying. "So he drove back here with you in the back of the truck?"

"I think he forgot I was in the back of the truck at first. When he remembered, it was too late, and he had to throw me in the woods. He left the blanket on my head."

Ida Gold stepped up into Lulu's face. "Bullshit!" She turned to Aunt Annie. "Bullshit!" Ida left Lulu and Aunt Annie to their reunion of lies.

Aunt Annie turned when one of her fiddler crabs stepped up next to her. He had seen the broken gate and the injured guard. "Aunt Annie, I'm sorry to interrupt your party, but someone ran the main gate and hurt Buster real bad. It's a mess out there. Mr. Phil took both men to the hospital. I ran back to let you know what happened."

"Take another man with you and get back out there. Nobody comes in, and nobody leaves without bein' cleared by you. Use them guns if you have to."

Officers Boos and Short were standing outside near the main house. The porch was filled with people trying to get inside to get close to Jack Jarvis. The two policemen were more at ease as they walked around. No one had challenged them or questioned their presence up to that point, so they had no reason to think they would be discovered at all. They had pulled off their infiltration of the criminal world on Black Hammock Island.

They knew something was wrong when a large number of Aunt Annie's armed guards gathered in front of the main house. Aunt Annie had given the word that there was a dangerous intruder who had killed Luther Rude. Aunt Annie walked out onto the front porch to direct her small army of fiddler crabs.

"Don't know much about this man. Be on the look out for a man walkin' alone. He's probably young and strong lookin'. Be careful, because the one thing we do know is that he is a bad man. Don't know much else. Investigate anything strange or out of place. Keep your eyes open."

Paul Short and David Boos stood in the crowd listening to Aunt Annie's mandate. They moved away so they could talk privately. Paul Short looked around to be sure they were alone. "I wonder who caused all this hoop-la."

David Boos shook his head. "I want to stay and see what's goin' on, but if we have to get involved, we'll blow our cover and then what? Let's just see if we can leave without a problem."

Fabian Moore stood behind Mary C. next to John King's 1957 Chevy. She did not hear or see him walk up on her. Her heart jumped when she recognized his voice.

"You really didn't think I was gonna let you come out here alone, did ya?"

Mary C. did not turn to face him at first. "You always act like you're gonna do what I say, and then you don't. Why is that?"

"You're the only mama I have, and I want to keep you and Jason around."

She turned to him. "To be such a bad ass, you sure talk like a sissy boy."

Fabian had to smile at Mary C.'s remark after he told her how he felt about their relationship. "You alright?"

Mary C. wanted to know about Rebecca. "You didn't let the girl go, did ya?"

"Everything's fine. The most important thing is gettin' us both out of here alive."

"You just let her go, didn't ya?"

"She'll be at my house when we get there. Rebecca or the necklace won't make no difference if we don't make it back home."

Mary C. was ready to deal with the matter at hand. "I need you to help me get upstairs in that house. You know I've got to take her down myself? She has to know it's me. Only you and me know what she did. I have to be the one who pulls the trigger. She'll have to come up there sometime. I'll wait 'til she does. Get me in that house."

Fabian wanted Mary C. to know what they were facing. "You know, all the commotion is because they're probably huntin' for me. It don't matter why; they just are."

Mary C. shook her head. "Maybe with all this confusion we can walk right through it all and march in the front door."

Fabian smiled. "Maybe so, but let's try the back door first."

Mary C. opened the car door and took out her pump action shotgun. She leaned it against the car.

Aunt Annie stood in the middle of the crowd gathered in the main house. Two armed guards stood next to her. "Ladies and gentlemen, it has come to our attention that we have an unwelcome intruder here on the island. He might be in this room right now." Everyone talked and looked around at the others in the room. "I'm askin' that y'all bear with us for a while. Go out and take advantage of our many activities. We need to clear this room."

Theda Moore did not care what was happening as long as she was with Jason. She also realized she liked watching sex being performed but not as much as she liked performing. Rebecca had taken some of Jason's attention, but he made sure he added Theda to the mix. He knew Rebecca Coolie was probably a short term deal when Theda was a long-term sexual companion. Jason was a smart young man when it came to women, or teenaged girls, in Theda's case. He made sure she was happy and an active participant.

Rebecca seemed to understand the sexual game as well. She was sure to cater to Theda's needs and let her have her turn. At ages fifteen and eighteen, the two young women were sexual veterans, and Jason was in heaven.

One time while Jason was kneeling behind Rebecca, Theda reached out and squeezed one of Rebecca's huge breasts. It was obvious she wanted to know what they actually felt like. Rebecca smiled and followed her lead. She reached out and touched one of Theda's breasts as Jason pounded her from behind. Theda smiled and kissed Rebecca on her cheek. When Rebecca touched Theda, Jason pumped hard. When Theda kissed Rebecca, Jason pumped even harder. He was trying to get an audible reaction from Rebecca, but so far she only moaned with delight. She was not a screamer like Theda. Not yet, anyway.

Theda's baby, Sammy, started crying in his crib down the hall. She started to get up out of the bed. Rebecca moved away from Jason. "I'll see to Sammy. You stay here."

Theda was surprised but pleased at Rebecca's offer. "Thank you."

Rebecca slid off the bed. Theda and Jason watched her naked body as she left the room. They couldn't help it. Jason grabbed Theda and turned her on her stomach. She screamed on Jason's second hard thrust into her body. Rebecca smiled when she heard Theda's wild, vocal reaction. Her stomach muscles contracted. She picked Sammy up out of his crib.

The majority of the crowd had left Aunt Annie's main house and gathered outside. Most of them went on to the other venues of entertainment, but there were some ready to leave the island now that the fight was over. The number of armed guards also made them nervous. If any shooting started, everyone was in danger of being hit by stray bullets. The crowd was getting restless at the thought they could not leave when they wanted.

Lulu Vesta was taking a hot bath upstairs. Ida Gold stood with Aunt Annie on the front porch. Aunt Annie addressed the multitude with her voice amplified through a megaphone she held up to her mouth. "There's been a big misunderstanding. I'm sorry about the confusion. You are free to leave whenever you wish. I would never make you stay. We do hope you'll spend more time with us, but if you can't this time, thank you for comin' and see ya next time. Please stop at the main gate--what's left of it--and allow the guards to be sure no stranger's hiding in your vehicle. Thank y'all for your cooperation." Aunt Annie had sent word to the gate guards to allow the customers to leave when they wanted but to be on the lookout for anything odd or suspicious.

The cars and trucks began to roll. With all the people going to their vehicles, it was the perfect time for Mary C. and Fabian to make their move toward the main house. They had decided to walk right through the people, trucks and cars and see just how far they could get. They walked side by side, and Fabian carried the shotgun down low next to his leg. They were only about fifty yards from the house. No one had given them a second look. They walked next to and behind moving cars and trucks for most of the distance. A number of the guards had to start directing the drivers as the first Black Hammock Island traffic jam began to form.

Jack Jarvis was in his room trying to come down from the excitement, so he could leave and end his stay on the evil island. He wanted to go to Mayport and collect that kiss Mary C. had promised him.

Theda's son, Sammy, lay on a blanket on the floor next to Theda's bed. The two young women had developed an almost tag team system to their sexual activity with Jason. Each time he exploded, they would give him time to recover by taking turns stimulating him orally until he was able to rise to the occasion. While one of the girl's hot lips were on him, he was using his tongue and fingers on the other. The threesome became a well-oiled sexual machine in a matter of two hours. Jason wanted the two young women to use their talents on each other as he watched, but they had only touched and kissed briefly. He was hoping it was just a matter of time before they were comfortable satisfying each other. He liked watching two women together. His experience with Ruby and Jessie in Cosmo and then Margie and Helga at the Giant's Motel had given him a taste. He wanted more. Jason saw the opportunity to make an exciting move for all of them.

Jason was lying on his back with Rebecca lying next to him, also flat on her back. The fingers on his right hand were moving in and out of her body. Theda was kneeling between Jason's legs stimulating him orally. Jason moved his right hand away from Rebecca and took Theda by her hair. He gently lifted her head, breaking her lip-lock suction on his manliness. Theda looked up at Jason and smiled. He moved her head over and placed it between Rebecca's legs. Theda knew what Jason wanted, and she was willing to please him no matter what. When Theda's tongue touched Rebecca, the audible reaction Jason was looking for from Rebecca bounced off the bedroom walls. She actually screamed her own banshee version, and little Sammy screamed with her. Jason grabbed himself, but it was too late. He exploded for the third time as he watched his companions get to know each other.

Mary C. and Fabian had made it all the way to the back of the main house without delay. There was one armed guard sitting in a chair next to the steps leading to the upstairs. He stood up and stepped forward. "You folks can't be back here." He looked down and saw the shotgun next to Fabian's leg. Before he could lift his rifle, Fabian's fast and lethal right hand hit the man in his throat. It was a similar blow to the one Jack Jarvis had inflicted on Grave Digger earlier that day in the ring. The difference with Fabian's blow was the guard ended up dead. He went down like a ton of bricks. Mary C.'s heart raced at the frightening speed and accuracy that Fabian possessed. Fabian picked up the guard and sat him back in the chair and placed the rifle across his lap. Mary C. had to ask.

"Is he dead?"

"As a door nail." Fabian led Mary C. up the back stairs.

The crowd downstairs was still clearing out, and Aunt Annie had not sent any guards upstairs. Fabian opened the door and saw no one in the hallway. He handed Mary C. his combat knife. "If you use this scatter gun, you'll never get out of here." Then he handed her his pistol. "If you have to fight your way out, use this as a last resort." She took both weapons. Fabian held the door open so Mary C. could enter the hallway. He left with the shotgun and went down the back steps. He lifted the guard out of the chair, moved him to the ground and rolled his body under in small platform porch. Fabian picked up the man's baseball cap that had fallen on the ground and put it on his own head. Then Fabian sat in the chair with the shotgun across his lap. He would try to wait for Mary C. to complete her revenge. He would also stop anyone who might try to use the back stairway.

Mary C. stood against the wall in the upstairs hallway. She was only two doors away from Aunt Annie's room. If she could just get to the room she would wait as long as she had to. She was surprised the hall was empty. There was the possibility someone was already in the bedroom, perhaps Aunt Annie herself. Someone flushed the toilet in the bathroom across from where Mary C. was standing. She knew someone would soon step out of that bathroom and see her in the hall. Mary C. had to move. She turned the doorknob to Aunt Annie's room, and the door opened. She was in the room in a second and closed the door. The room was not occupied.

Whoever was in the bathroom entered the hallway. The sound of footsteps on the hall floor stopped at the door of Aunt Annie's room. Mary C. knew she was going to have a visitor. Her heart raced again as she put the huge combat knife on the floor. She reached into her pants pocket and took out the Black Jack her friend Skinny Millington had given her and taught her to use. She had used it to incapacitate James Thorn in the East Mayport woods near the Indian mounds. She was only there to kill Aunt Annie. She had to be sure Aunt Annie was going to open that door. Mary C. moved to the wall, so when the door opened it would hide her until it was closed again. It would give her a few seconds to zero in on her possible victim.

The door swung open and pinned Mary C. to the wall for a brief moment. As the door closed Mary C. recognized one of Aunt Annie's lovers. Lulu Blondie Vesta had entered the room. She was wrapped in a towel. Her back was to Mary C., and she was an easy and perfect target for swinging the Black Jack. Lulu never saw it coming as the leather-covered steel slapped her in the back of her head. She fell so hard and fast that Mary C. was worried she had killed her anyway. If she wasn't dead, she sure wasn't waking up anytime too soon. Mary C. settled in to wait for Aunt Annie to be the next one to walk through the door.

Mr. King stood on the porch of his haunted house. He looked toward Miss Margaret's store. There was a woman standing on the near side of the building. For a moment, the earlier talk of Anna Jo Hamilton made him visualize her as the lone woman at the store.

He shook the impossible thought from his head. Mr. King focused in on the dark figure and thought he recognized her, but he wasn't sure. A second hard look revealed to him it was Stella Croom, Joe's mother. She was just standing there staring at his house. He walked down the porch steps and turned toward her. When she realized he was walking in her direction, she stepped quickly to the back of the building and was gone.

Mr. King went into the store. Peggy and Susan were on duty. They were cleaning, stocking and waiting on customers when they came shopping. They both turned to the door when Mr. King came in and the bell rang.

"Good afternoon, ladies."

The two sisters were in stereo. "Good afternoon, Mr. King. May we help you with something?"

"Was Miss Stella, Joe Croom's mama, just in the store?"

The girls looked at each other. "No, sir."

Mr. King nodded his head. "Y'all got any BC powder? I got a headache to die from."

Jack Jarvis had packed his small duffle bag and was ready to leave. He was relaxing and waiting for the traffic jam to thin out. The horns had stopped blowing, and the people had stopped yelling. The traffic was moving along at a steady pace. With only one road in or out of the island, it was a slow process when so many cars left at the same time.

There was a knock on the door. Mary C. heard it, too. Jack opened the door to find Aunt Annie standing in the hall. Mary C. had no idea how close her victim was at that very moment.

"I was hopin' ya hadn't left yet, Mr. Jarvis. With all that's goin' on 'round here, I wouldn't blame ya if you just took off without sayin' good-bye."

"I wouldn't do that, ma'am."

"No, sir, I guess not. A damn fighter with manners, if that don't take the cake." She handed Jack a thick white envelope. "I'm sure you wouldn't leave without collectin' this, now would ya?" Jack took the envelope and stuffed it in the back pocket of his pants. "You ain't gonna count it?"

"No, ma'am. I'm sure it's all there."

"You are full of surprises, Mr. Jarvis. I want to thank you for your performance out there today. It was a great day for the island. I'm sorry this foolishness put a little damper on the day. You sure did surprise us all out there. You're one hell of a man."

"Well, I don't know about that, but thanks for sayin' it."

Aunt Annie wanted more from him. "You and Mary C. got pretty friendly didn't y'all?

Jack did not like the question at all. "I guess so." He hated Aunt Annie for what she had done to Mary C. He did not know all the details, but he hated her for the little he did know.

"One of my boys got sliced up like a pig here last night. You didn't see nothin' out of the ordinary, did ya?"

"Can't say I did, but I was sleepin' pretty hard."

Aunt Annie smiled. "A man like you don't sleep hard, Mr. Jarvis. Hell, you probably don't sleep at all. That's why ya stay so mean inside. Lack of sleep makes ya mean." She sat down in one of the chairs. "I know for a fact you stayed up pretty late humpin' with Mary C. Ain't much goes on 'round here I don't know 'bout."

Jack was tired of the game. "Aunt Annie, I'm gonna leave now. Thank you for the opportunity to fight here and earn the money." He picked his bag up off of the floor and moved to the door.

Aunt Annie was crazy. "What do ya think happened to Mary C. when she left you here last night?"

Jack stopped at the door. "I'm not sure what you want me to say, but I don't like the tone you're using."

"How 'bout this tone, then. Mr. Jarvis, when she left you, I tied Mary C. to a bed in a hell hole. The most vile and nasty man I've ever seen in my nasty and vile life paid top dollar to violate her as he pleased. As you have already learned, I usually don't have no rules, but I did have one about Mary C. That good ol' boy could do whatever he wanted, as long as he didn't kill her. That's gonna be my job." Jack's blood was boiling inside his body as the she-man continued. "I only got one man in there last night, but it was gonna go on for days, maybe weeks. Then after just one nasty man, somebody helped her get away before I could cut her into pieces and feed her to my dogs. I have fed human flesh to my dogs. It makes 'em wild fighters. They fight like you." She stood up from the chair. "I didn't think about you 'til I saw you hit that poor bastard in the ring. Did you take Mary C. away so you could keep her for ya self?"

Jack walked out the door without responding to her last question. He closed the door and turned to walk toward the stairs leading to the big room downstairs. He saw someone in his peripheral vision. Jack turned to defend himself and came eye to eye with Mary C. She put her index finger to her mouth, so he would not talk. She pointed to the door of the room and whispered, "Annie?" Jack nodded. She pointed toward the back door leading to the stairway and whispered again. "Go that way." He looked down at the pistol stuck in her pants. Jack Jarvis left Mary C. to deal with Aunt Annie.

Aunt Annie's head was down, and she was talking to herself when she pushed the bedroom door open. She was planning to follow Jack Jarvis and continue her abusive and revealing conversation downstairs. Aunt Annie was hoping he would get angry enough and explode and possibly give her information she needed. Aunt Annie did not see the Black Jack until it landed on the bridge of her nose. Her nose exploded, with blood gushing instantly. She staggered back into the room. She had no choice. Mary C. closed the door as Aunt Annie stood in front of her dazed from the blow. Mary C. swung the leather again hitting Aunt Annie in the mouth, shattering four of her upper front teeth.

Aunt Annie towered above Mary C., but she could not defend herself against the brutal attack. Mary C. dropped the Black Jack to the floor and held the combat knife in her hand. One hard swing sent the huge blade into the left side of Aunt Annie's neck. The sharp point of the knife went all the way through to the right side. Mary C. jerked the knife out allowing the serrated edge to cut again, leaving a gaping gash on both sides of Aunt Annie's neck. The big woman went down to her knees. She did not make a sound as she stared in shock at her assassin. Mary C. stepped back so Aunt Annie could see her better.

"Can ya see me, Annie?" Aunt Annie only stared forward. "Come on, now. Nod your ugly head if you know who I am. I wanted to tell you earlier that you were an idiot, but I just knew I'd get the opportunity again. You are really an idiot." Mary C. picked up the Black Jack off the floor. "Can't leave this little goodie behind." She patted it in her hand the same way she did when she used it on James Thorn. Mary C. had a mental flashback of her comment to James Thorn after she hit him with the Black Jack. She thought it was rather appropriate at that particular moment. "Boy, this thing really knocks the shit out ya, don't it?"

Mary C. had to smile at her repeating the sarcastic and hateful phrase. Aunt Annie's body fell forward and slammed to the floor. Mary C.'s heart beat even harder when she knew she had accomplished her mission of Mary C. justice. She talked out loud to her victim one more time. "Damn, I hope you knew it was me."

Jack Jarvis stood with Fabian Moore. Fabian was still sitting in the chair. They recognized each other when Jack came out the door and down the stairs. Fabian had told him briefly of Mary C.'s intentions. Jack told Fabian that Mary C. was with Aunt Annie at that very moment. They both looked up the steps hoping Mary C. would join them at any second. As they waited, two armed workers walked near them about twenty yards away. They both recognized Jack Jarvis so he waved. "Thought I'd sneak out the back door. I don't think I can sign another ass today."

One of the men yelled back. "I wish I had that problem. Great fight, Mr. Jarvis." Jack nodded as the men walked on by. They never even noticed Fabian sitting in the chair.

Mary C. stood at the bedroom door mentally preparing to make her run for the back door. She heard footsteps in the hall as someone passed the room. She opened the door just wide enough to see Ida Crew Cut Gold across the hall, walking into Aunt Annie's bedroom. Mary C. knew she would find Blondie knocked out on the floor. Mary C. opened the door and walked quickly into the other room. The door was wide open, and Ida Gold was standing there looking down at Lulu. Mary C. was preparing to use the Black Jack on the muscular Ida Gold. Her back was to Mary C., but she turned to face her when she heard the door close behind her. Ida's reaction was much quicker than Mary C. had anticipated. They were face to face, a situation Mary C. had not planned for. Ida saw the leather Black Jack in Mary C.'s hand. Ida Crew Cut Gold had no fear in her eyes. She even seemed to revel in the possibilities of a physical confrontation with the legend.

"You think you gonna hit me with that head buster? I hope you ain't alone, cause you've made a real big mistake." She looked

down at Lulu. "You did do me a favor if she's dead. Lyin' bitch."
Ida smiled and pulled a straight razor from the back pocket of her
pants. She opened the razor, and it actually shone for a second as
she turned it toward the light. Mary C. knew Ida was right about her
making a mistake and not attacking from behind. Mary C. also
knew Ida Gold was stronger. She did not have time or the ability for
hand to hand combat with the butch wax lesbian. Ida's eyes showed
fear for the first time when Mary C. pulled out Fabian's pistol,
pointed it at Ida and pulled the trigger. Mary C. hit Ida with four
bullets at close range before she stopped pulling the trigger. Three
of the projectiles hit Ida in her chest, and one hit her dead center on
her chin.

Fabian jumped up when he heard the shots. Jack looked up the
stairs. They both knew everyone within a hundred yards heard the
distinctive sound of gun fire. Fabian ran up the stairs to rescue
Mary C. His mind set was for war. Jack Jarvis followed him.
Fabian was only a few steps from the top when the door flew open
and Mary C. came out of the building. She knew using the gun had
created big trouble for them all. As she moved past Fabian, she
offered an explanation.

"Sorry. I was gonna take a real ass-wipin'. It was definitely a
last resort." She moved past Jack Jarvis. "Hey, Jack. Ain't got
time for that kiss."

Three guards ran down the hallway checking the rooms. They
found Aunt Annie first and then Ida Gold and Lulu Vesta. The
guard that checked Lulu found she was still alive and only
unconscious. He remained with her to administer first-aid while the
other two men left to alert the others of their findings.

CHAPTER SEVEN

Officers Paul Short and David Boos had both armed themselves when they heard the gun shots. They reached the edge of the house when Jack, Fabian and Mary C. came running around the corner. They all stopped and stared at each other. Before anyone could say a word about the strange meeting, five armed men ran out of the house. One of the men yelled, "There they are! They killed Aunt Annie!" The guards began firing their guns. David Boos felt a bullet hit the leg of his pants. He returned the fire and hit one of the men in his thigh, dropping him to the ground.

Fabian pushed Jack. "Get Mary C. to the car and get her out of here!" Bullets were whizzing through the air. Paul Short and David Boos took cover on the side of the building. Fabian dove behind a car and Jack Jarvis shielded Mary C. with his body and moved her away from the battle.

David Boos looked at Paul Short as flying bullets splintered pieces of wood on the side of the house. They both saw Mary C. running away with Jack Jarvis. It would have been hard for them to believe Mary C. was there if they had not seen her with their own eyes. Both policemen sat on the ground behind the side of the building. The good old boys in Aunt Annie's fiddler crab army were excellent hunters, but the prey never shot back. They were not as willing to move forward with fire being returned and bullets coming back in their direction. They were also looking for a safe hiding place. David Boos had to speak his mind while the gun fire stopped for a moment.

"You do realize we're covering for Mary C. as she gets away, don't ya? It's like we're on the same side if we want to be or not. If we get out of this alive, please tell me how this happened."

Paul Short shook his head. "We ain't got much choice, do we? What do ya think she's doin' here, anyway? This is too crazy. The soldier's with her, and she's with the fighter. This is way too crazy. Who the hell is she?"

Even with bullets flying all around, David Boos still had to share more thoughts. "You can bet your sweet ass somebody's dead, if not more than one. From the way they're actin', it's probably Aunt Annie. Can't say I'd be sad about that one." His mind went back to Mary C. "You know she just about drove Mr. Butler crazy. Hell, she probably did drive him crazy. But, I ain't lettin' her drive me crazy. If we get back alive, I'm thowin' that damn book of his with the list in it away." More gunshots ended Officer Boos' thoughts about Mary C.'s ability to alter a man's mind.

Fabian had not fired a shot. The shotgun was for close range, and the fiddler crabs were too far away for the shotgun pellets to do much damage. He was at a serious disadvantage with the other men having long range rifles. Fabian smiled when he looked to his left and saw Mr. King's 1957 Chevy roll out onto the one road. He knew Mary C. was leaving Black Hammock Island.

Jack Jarvis waved to Fabian and disappeared behind some trees. Jack was hoping to get to his car and meet Mary C. at the Mayport ferry. Fabian was not giving the two policemen a second thought. He knew it was every man for himself, and he was sure they knew that, too. The only thing on Fabian's mind was to get to the truck and follow Mary C. The small army of fiddler crabs had gone from five to fifteen shooters. The odds were becoming way out of proportion.

A silver LP gas cylinder fuel tank leaned against the outside wall of the house with copper tubing leading in the building for heat and cooking. Most of the shooters were into that particular area of the yard. Fabian whistled to get the policemen's attention. David Boos looked first. Fabian held up his shotgun. "Shoot the damn fuel tank. I can't reach it with this."

David Boos looked around the corner of the house and saw the tank Fabian was so interested in. He looked at Paul Short. "What do ya think?"

"It might cause enough hell to give us time to get to the car. They're gonna flush us out. We can't stay here much longer. We gotta do somethin'. I ain't got no better idea."

David Boos reloaded his gun. "If it blows, we go."

Fabian could see the officers preparing to take a shot at the gas tank. He was ready to move, too. Officer Boos fired the first shot hitting the tank dead center. Nothing happened. All the fiddler crabs ducked down when they heard the shot. David's second shot was a completely different story. The tank exploded, sending metal pieces and a ball of fire into the air and into the side of the main house. The flames grabbed each slat of wood one at a time. The old dry planks on the house caught fire like a pile of dead cedar Christmas trees. The side of the main house was covered in flames in a matter of seconds. The armed fiddler crabs were running to get clear of the fire and debris. No one was thinking about shooting anybody.

As soon as the fireball went up, Fabian was on the move. The two officers knew it was time for their move, also. Four men had run in their direction when the fire ball first went up. The two officers left the safety of their cover and suddenly found themselves just thirty yards away from the four men. They all froze as they looked at each other. Paul Short had to give it a try. He pulled out his badge and yelled, "Police! Drop your weapons!" All four workers raised their weapons and fired at the officers. Either they did not hear Officer Short, or they did not care about his request. The two officers returned fire and ran toward the cars as the bullets hit all around them. Once again David Boos had to express his thought as he ran along side of his partner. "Did you just say, 'Police, drop your weapons'?"

Paul Short smiled as they ran, "Hell, I thought I'd give it a shot."

Fabian jumped into the truck and started the engine. As he pressed down the gas pedal, he felt the back bed of the truck shake when the two police officers jumped in. Fabian smiled as the truck roared out onto the main road leading off of the island. He smiled again when he looked through the front windshield and saw Jack

Jarvis standing on the side of the road. Fabian slowed the truck down while Jack Jarvis joined the two policemen in the back bed of the truck. He sat down and nodded to Paul and David.

"Couldn't find my car. Mary C. owes me a kiss."

The fiddler crabs had turned their attention to the destructive fire that had engulfed the main house on Black Hammock Island. They could only watch it burn. No one was going to run back into the burning building to carry out Aunt Annie's or Ida Gold's body.

Lulu Vesta stood with a group of the women who lived on the island. She had a bandage on her head from the black jack Mary C. swung so effectively. For a brief moment she wondered how it would feel to be called Aunt Lulu.

There was chaos at the front gate, or what was left of it. Only one car was leaving, and the guards were concerned with the awful explosion they had heard. The last car drove out onto the main road, and the two guards turned to look down the road when they heard the sound of an engine moving fast. The truck came into their sight, and they knew it was not going to stop at the gate. Both men positioned themselves on each side of the road with plans to take out the driver and anyone else in the vehicle.

Fabian saw the guards moving ahead. He knocked on the back window but kept his eyes on the road and the guards. "We ain't gone yet, fellas. We got company. You'll have to take 'em before they shoot at me first. Stay down. I'll say when." The three in the back of the truck went low and waited for Fabian's call.

"There's one on both sides, and I don't think we can stop and try to reason with 'em." Fabian saw the guards raise their rifles. "Take 'em boys!"

The guard on the left side fired first. The bullet hit the front windshield and whizzed right out the back window. Paul Short's first shot grazed the guard's ear, but the second bullet took him out when it hit him in his eye. The other guard got a number of rapid shots off; one hit the front windshield and the other hit the side panel of the truck and ricocheted off. David Boos' first shot hit the second guard in his shoulder knocking him back into the ditch. The truck went through the uncovered entrance and fishtailed out on to the main road. All three men in the back of the truck were tossed about as Fabian got control of the truck and headed toward the Mayport ferry. Jack Jarvis was grateful for the two officer's sharp shooting abilities.

"Good shootin', gentlemen. I sure didn't want to die in that hell hole."

Paul Short nodded as they all felt the truck slowing down. Fabian pulled the truck to the side of the road and stopped. David Boos looked back down the road to be sure no one was following them. There was nothing coming their way. He turned back to Paul Short and gave a half smile of relief. Paul had a strange look on his face. He turned and looked into the back window of the truck. David's eyes widened when he saw that Fabian Moore was not at the wheel. His body had fallen down into the seat. They both jumped from the back seat, and each opened one of the truck doors.

Fabian lay on his side. His eyes were wide open, but had no life in them at all. One of the bullets from the guards had hit the desired target. Another young Mayport man with ties to Mary C. was dead. Officer Boos and Officer Short looked at each other. They both knew what the other was thinking.

Margie sat in her bedroom looking at the carousel music box. She wasn't ready for another fairy tale sexual encounter. Her dreams were becoming more and more frightening and bazaar. There was a knock on her bedroom door. Her sister Susan and new partner in sexually double teaming Jason wanted to talk. Margie left the music box out so Susan could see it. "Come on in; it's open."

Susan walked in and looked right at the carousel. She was excited. "What are you doing? Did you use it today?"

"You might say that."

"What happened?"

"You won't believe me, and you'll laugh. I know you think I'm crazy already. If I tell you, you'll really think I'm nuts."

"No, I won't, either. I promise."

Margie realized something. "You've been using the carousel, haven't you?"

Susan put her head down, and then looked at Margie. "I couldn't help it. I just couldn't. You started all this with us two being with Jason. I think about it all the time. I just wanted to know what you know. It scares me though. Aren't you afraid of it?"

Margie had to agree. "I wasn't at first, but the dreams are different now. It's like a mixture of what we think during the time before we turn it on. My last dream was scary, but stupid, too."

"Tell me what it was."

Margie looked into Susan's eyes. "If you laugh, I will never tell you another thing."

Susan sat down on the edge of the bed. "I promise I won't laugh."

The Mayport ferry was floating into the docking slip at the same time Mary C. saw Jason's truck coming toward her. Her heart jumped when she realized Fabian was safe and joining her for the ferry ride back to Mayport. She saw there were others with him and had to smile as the truck came closer and she recognized Officers Short and Boos sitting in the back of the truck. The thought that they had fought with Fabian and then had to escape in the truck with him was a humorous situation and strange turn of events. She knew the two proud lawmen did not like the outcome of their visit to Black Hammock Island. She also knew they were part of it now and couldn't do too much about it. They had not really seen her do anything illegal, and as a friend of Jack Jarvis, she would just tell them she and Fabian were there to see her friend Jack fight and they started shooting at her. Her smile was even bigger as the truck drove into the ferry parking area. The truck stopped where she was standing.

Mary C. stepped to the driver's side door to greet her young hero. She was taken aback but pleased to see Jack Jarvis at the wheel of the truck. "Jack, what are you ..." She looked past him and did not see Fabian. An awful feeling poured over her body. She looked at Jack.

Jack's facial expression told her something was wrong. "He's in the back."

Mary C. continued staring at Jack. She knew she did not want to look in the back of that truck. Hot liquid filled her throat as her stomach soured. She was still looking at Jack.

"I'm sorry, Mary C."

She turned away from the window and her eyes met with David Boos'. He looked down as a non-verbal direction to Fabian's body. Mary C. did not look at Fabian. Her eyes did burn a hole into David

Boos' soul. She walked away from the truck and got back into Mr. King's 1957 Chevy, started the engine, and waited for the ferry worker to wave them across the ramp and onto the big car carrier.

Susan had fallen off of Margie's bed onto the floor as she roared with laughter. Margie's colorful explanation of her seven dwarf orgy was just too much for her sister to take.

Margie was disgusted. "Oh now, that's real nice of you! Susan, you promised."

Susan tried to talk through her hysterical belly laugh. "I know I promised, but I wasn't ready to hear about how big Dopey's *thing* was. Margie could not help herself. She burst into laughter and joined Susan on the floor.

The marathon sex event at the Moore house was over. One of the willing participants, Theda Moore, stood in her kitchen wearing only her panties. She was making sandwiches for the hungry sexual threesome. Jason was with her wearing only his dungarees and holding her baby, Sammy, in his arms. Jason smiled and looked down the hall where he could hear the shower running in the bathroom. Rebecca Milkduds Coolie had made herself at home. She was taking a shower. Jason moved away from the kitchen and walked to the bathroom door. He still held Sammy as he pushed open the bathroom door.

Jason could see Rebecca's shapely silhouette through the thin plastic shower curtain. Rebecca turned off the shower and pulled the curtain back to see Jason standing there. She smiled and reached for a towel. Jason watched her dry the water from her body. Rebecca put on a slow enticing show as she turned, rubbed and bent her body in every direction. She knew Jason did not want to talk. He only wanted to watch. At eighteen-years-old, Rebecca Coolie was a true pleaser in every sense of the word.

Susan had talked Margie into turning on the magic carousel. Her rationale was that if they were together, perhaps they could protect each other. Margie knew it was a weak reasoning, but she needed an excuse to use the music box again. She was addicted, and it looked like her sister would also soon be a sexual dream addict as well. Margie made sure her bedroom door was locked and pushed the *on* switch of the antique music box.

Rebecca walked into the kitchen wrapped in a towel. Theda turned to see her with Jason and Sammy standing behind her. Rebecca smiled. "Can I borrow a pair of panties? I ain't got no clothes at all."

"In my room, top drawer, right side." Theda put the sandwiches on the table as Rebecca left the room. She looked at Jason. "Here, I know you must be hungry."

Jason smiled and walked over to Theda. It surprised her when he put his free hand around her waist and pulled her to him. Her bare breasts pushed against him. Sammy was pinned between them as Jason still held the child. Jason kissed Theda with the most passionate and meaningful kiss she had ever experienced from him. It was real and full of caring and affection. It took her heart and breath away. It was a kiss she would feel forever. Nothing else would ever matter. She would be in love with Jason for the rest of her long life.

Rebecca walked back into the kitchen as the one-of-a-kind kiss ended. She knew that the young Theda Moore had been able to steal a piece of Jason's heart. Rebecca wore only Theda's panties, too. She knew Jason would like that, and perhaps he would be a buffer between her and Mary C. when the time came for the big one on one meeting with the devil woman. She was hoping that with Fabian's feelings for her and Jason's lust, she just might have a chance to survive her next adventure.

Susan's carousel philosophy about the two sister's being able to protect each other went out the window when she found herself alone in the dark as the hypnotic lights and music took her away. "Margie, where are you?" She saw and heard nothing. "Please say you're here with me." Again, there was nothing. Susan knew she had made a big mistake. She did see movement in the dark ahead of her as her eyes adjusted to the lack of light. "Margie, is that you?"

A raspy voice sent a chill through her body. "No, not Margie, but an old friend of hers. I knew I'd get to you sooner or later. My goal is to be like Jason and be with all four sisters. Real or dream, it doesn't matter to me. I've been a Dream Walker for as long as I can remember. I won't hurt you, but just a little bit. I do promise the pain you feel will be most enjoyable. The best thing is that you can say it was a dream, so it ain't your fault. We both get what we want." Susan knew the midget, Tom Thumb, from the Giant's Motel was the talker from the dark. She had not seen him yet, but she knew.

"Why would you think we would both get what we wanted? I don't want to be with you."

"That doesn't matter. You want a sexual adventure, something different, a change from what you know. And it's guilt free, exactly what you four sisters are looking for. You want to do 'the nasty', but you want to hide your deep dark desires. This is perfect for you. No guilt. What a wonderful thing."

The midget walked out of the dark. He was completely naked with other naked men lined up behind him. Susan looked at his oversized male member as it stood up and pointed at her like a divining rod. Her eyes were wide open as Little Tom smiled an ugly and evil grin. "You can either turn around and bend over or open that mouth and say 'ahh.' There is no wrong choice for you to make."

Mary C. drove up to the front porch of Mr. King's haunted house. He was not sitting in his usual favorite spot. She got out of the 1957 Chevy as Jack Jarvis drove the truck up behind it. Officers Boos and Short jumped out of the back bed of the truck, and Jack Jarvis joined them. Mary C. was on the top step looking back at the three men. Officer Boos addressed her.

"We need to get the body to the station. Can we take the truck so we don't have to move him again?" Mary C. nodded her head. David Boos continued. "We'll bring the truck back when we get more men to go back and get our car and see what's left to do on the island." He looked at Jack Jarvis. "You need to get your car, too, don't ya?"

Jack Jarvis shook his head. "Not if they gonna start shootin' again. They can keep that clunker. I'll get me another junk yard special. In my line of work you never drive a nice car. Folks get mad when they lose their money, and they've been known to take it out on my car. No, I ain't goin' back out there."

Mr. King walked out of the house and walked up behind Mary C. His heart sank deep when he saw Fabian's dead body in the back of the truck. "Oh, dear God, not our Fabian."

Margie was into her part of the carousel hypnotic dream. There were no fairy tale characters, no long line of naked men, no midget hooked to her leg. Her dream was to be the spectator as she watched her sister Susan be pounded and pummeled from behind by man after man. Susan screamed in fright and pain as the perverted onslaught continued for the duration of the dream. Margie could only watch. She could not help her sister. A light flashed in Margie's eyes, and she lost sight of Susan. When she focused again, Susan was gone. She heard a noise behind her. It was the midget. Margie screamed when his huge pointer came at her like a 3-D movie.

"Your turn, Mud Dobber!"

The carousel stopped spinning. Margie woke up. She was trembling at first, but relieved when she didn't have to stay in the dream and deal with the nasty little man. She focused her eyes on Susan lying naked on the bedroom floor in the fetal position. Margie covered her with a blanket and gave her time to recover from her latest turn with the magic music box from the collection at the Giant's Motel.

Jason, Theda and Rebecca were sitting at the kitchen table eating the sandwiches Theda had made. They stared at each other over the bread as they each took bites of their individual sandwich. Rebecca had an amusing thought. "After we get a little nourishment, maybe we can go again." Each one burst into laughter at the same time. Jason thought it was a pretty good idea.

Mary C. was taking a hot shower. The two police officers had taken the truck and gone to deliver Fabian's body to the morgue and report their findings. Jack Jarvis and Mr. King sat on the front porch. Mr. King was talking.

"This is a sad day. We've had a lot of those here lately. Thought they might be over, but I was wrong. I want to thank you for helpin' Mary C. She seems to need help now and then, even though she thinks she's invincible."

"She's some interesting woman, I can say that, and I've only known her a little over twenty-four hours. They did some bad stuff to her on that island, but she made 'em pay for it dearly."

"That sounds like our Mary C."

"I'm sorry about Fabian. He was one hell of a man."

Mr. King looked away from Jack Jarvis as his attention was taken by a man walking past the house on the main road. Mr. King knew right away the man was a stranger to Mayport. He was dressed in an old Navy blue suit with a white shirt and black bow tie. The shirt was dirty and stained, and the suit coat and pants were torn in places with the dust from the road. At first, Mr. King thought the man was a walking preacher, spreading the word of the gospel. When the man stopped in front of the house, Mr. King got a better look at the stranger. His face was lined by age and alcohol. Mr. King knew what he wanted.

"Y'all wouldn't have a dime so I could ride the ferry to the other side, would ya?"

Jack Jarvis surprised Mr. King when he stepped up and responded. "Where ya headed?"

"Anywhere, nowhere, here. I just keep movin'."

Jack reached into his pants pocket and took out a wad of money. He took a five dollar bill from the roll. "Here ya go, old timer. Get something to eat before ya buy your next bottle."

The man took the money. "Bless ya, young man. Don't run into folks like you too often."

Jack nodded. "I hope you'll eat somethin' first."

"I'll do just that." The man nodded to Mr. King and walked away toward Miss Margaret's store. Jack and Mr. King sat back down in the porch chairs.

Mary C. walked out onto the front porch. She was wearing the robe John had given her when she first moved into his haunted house. Mr. King really couldn't remember who left it there nor where it came from, but it was a ladies robe, and it was in one of the closets. The silk material was clinging to her curvaceous body. Jack Jarvis stood up from his chair. "Sit down, Jack. It's nice, but you don't have to be so formal with me." Jack sat back down in his seat and Mary C. plopped down in the chair next to him. She crossed her muscular legs exposing her skin when the slit in the front of the robe opened a few inches. Mary C. dripped of sexual magnetism at all times. It was one of her many gifts. She looked toward the street and saw the man walking away.

"Who's that, John?"

"Just another drifter asking for money to make it another day. He ain't the first or the last. Wanted a dime, but got five dollars from Mr. Jarvis here." Mr. King looked toward the store as the man walked in. "Looks like he might be getting somethin' to eat, Mr. Jarvis."

Mary C. smiled at Jack. "Smells like somethin's burnin' out here."

Mr. King lifted his nose into the air and took a deep breath. "I can't never smell nothing. Maybe somebody's burning trash."

Peggy turned to the door as the drifter walked into the front of the store. "Good afternoon. May I help you with something?"

He looked up at her and liked what he saw. "I didn't expect to see a beautiful woman in this town, but here you are."

His compliment made Peggy uneasy as he moved closer to her. "You got any gin here?"

"No, sir, we don't."

"How much for a kiss?"

Peggy's heart pounded with fear at his question. "We don't sell kisses here either, sir."

"That's too bad, 'cause a woman like you could make a bunch of money if ya did. If I stay in your little town for a while, maybe you'll change your mind. I hope to see ya again." Peggy did not respond. He turned toward the door. She was hoping he would leave. Her heart raced even harder when he turned back to face her again.

"I got five dollars, here." He patted his shirt pocket. "It's all yours if ya give me that kiss."

Peggy was frozen with fear. She wanted to scream and run out of the store, but her trembling legs said "no." She thought she was going to pass out when the man reached out, took her by the wrist, and pulled her to him. She was against him, and he grabbed the back of her head, kissing her as hard as he could. His whiskers rubbed her face. His breath was salty-hot, and he had an unusual odor to him. It was a mixture of smells dominated by burnt wood or maybe charcoal. His arm held her waist, squeezing the breath from her body. He squeezed one of her young hard breasts with his free hand and then moved the same hand down and rubbed her between her legs on the outside of her shorts.

Peggy wanted to scream for help, but there was no noise coming from her throat. She felt his hand move up the leg of her shorts. He worked his dirty fingers underneath her panties and pushed a single digit inside her. She made a whimpering noise at the discomfort of his dry entry. As his fingers groped and penetrated, her body fluids came to her rescue and his delight.

"That's it, girly. I knew you'd like it. I can tell you've done this before." He pulled his hand from under her panties. He released his arm from around her waist. Peggy moved away. Her eyes widened when the man unzipped his pants and took his organ into his hand. Peggy looked down as he held it toward her. It was her first experience with an uncircumcised penis. She continued her stare as the man pulled and stroked himself until his nasty juices erupted onto the floor from his ugly member.

Mary C. looked at Jack Jarvis and smiled. "Did John tell you this is a haunted house?"

Jack looked at Mr. King. "No, he didn't. I've been telling him about what happened today."

Mr. King looked at Mary C. "You should have told me. I'd a gone with you."

"That's just why I didn't tell ya. I didn't want you or Jason gettin' killed tryin' to protect me. Hell, I had the Jackal, our Fabian, a one-man killin' machine, and even two lawmen who showed up to lend me a hand. I was fine." She shook her head. "I don't know what those two were doin' out there, but I know they hated helpin' me get away. And then they rode back in my truck. If that ain't a hoot, I'll kiss your ass."

Jack smiled. "Mr. King, she's being kind by adding me to her line up of heroes. I didn't do much but help her get to her car. I have a feeling she could have done that little trick without me."

"Well, I know you were with Fabian the night he saved me. I know you were shot at, because you were helping me, and I know you beat the hell out of Grave Digger. Those three things I do know for a fact." She turned to Mr. King. "This man hits like a mule kicks."

John smiled. "I don't mean to change the subject, but I need to go tell Theda about Fabian. I don't know how she's gonna be able to take this horrible news. She's lost so much in a short amount of time. A young woman like her can just take so much."

"You go on and tell her, John. And tell that Coolie girl if she leaves again, I will hunt her down like I did this time. She's supposed to be there with Theda. She promised Fabian she'd go there, and she told me she had the necklace."

Mr. King's eyes lit up. "Are you serious?"

"She's got it, John. I knew it the whole time."

Mr. King stood up and walked to his car. "I'll be back."

He got into his car and drove toward Theda Moore's house. He saw the drifter leaving the store as he drove by. Mr. King did not like strangers walking on the streets of his beloved Mayport. His experiences with drifters and strangers were never of a positive nature. The beautiful face of the witch, Anna Jo, flashed in his head.

Mary C. took Jack Jarvis by his hand and walked him into the haunted house. She stopped at the foot of the stairs and kissed him like they had been life-long lovers. She wanted to push her body through his. Mary C. forced her pelvic area against his to the extent it was a tad painful. Jack knew she was naked under the robe; he had seen her nipples sticking to the material when they were on the porch. He reached inside the robe and touched one of her breasts. Mary C. drove her firm flesh into his strong and lethal hand. He squeezed hard, but she didn't care. He couldn't do it too hard. She reached down and rubbed him on the outside of his pants. Jack took her lead and reached under her robe to touch her the same way. As soon as his fingers found her, she was dripping wet and filled his hand with her hot body fluid. Instantly, he had two of his big fingers inside her and almost lifted her off the floor as he pulled his hand upward to go deeper. Mary C.'s hand was in his pants, grabbing and groping to free what she desired. She held him in her hand, and he felt the cool air touch his skin. His member was pleasing to her eyes, and she moved him into the living room where she pushed him into one of the chairs.

When Mary C. sat down across Jack's lap, the moisture between her legs allowed him to slide deep inside her with one movement. She pushed down as if she would pin him to the chair permanently. Jack Jarvis had never had more of a woman in his powerful arms than he had at that moment, and he knew it. He couldn't believe during one of the most erotic moments of his life he had to ask a question. "Is this house really haunted?"

Mary C. stopped for a second. "Like a graveyard." She continued her slow sexual motion.

Susan was sitting in the bedroom with Margie next to her. She was mentally exhausted from the awful sex dream. "I'm not doing it anymore. I must be going crazy to even try it the second time. How about we just do the real thing with Jason like before? I can't stop thinking about it, can you?"

"I think about it, but we can't just get the opportunity. That's why we fool with the carousel. It has made some great dreams, but lately they haven't been too much fun. I think we have to have more pleasant thoughts before we turn it on."

"I don't care what kind of thoughts we should have; I'm not doing it again."

Margie looked at her sister. "I saw what happened to you in the dream. That was my dream--to watch you." Susan's eyes widened. "It's true. I saw the whole thing. When they were finished with you, the midget came for me, but the carousel stopped, and the dream ended before he could get to me."

Susan was shocked. "Did you hear him say he was a Dream Walker?"

"Yes, I did."

"This is too scary, now, Margie. We have to get rid of that thing. I'm afraid one of us will get lost in there and not come back. Give it back to Jason. It really belongs to him. He's the one who brought it here in the first place. Or give it to Mary C. Didn't you say how much she liked it?"

Margie shook her head. "I think she got scared of it, too. She's the one who took it back to the Giant's Motel."

Susan shook her head, too. "And then you brought it back here."

Rebecca Coolie and Theda Moore ran to the back of the house when they heard a knock on the front door. They had to get their shirts on. Jason smiled as they scrambled out of the kitchen and down the hall. He went to see who was on the front porch.

Peggy was in shock over her ordeal with the drifter. Her fear and shame had her mind in a confused state. She was mopping up the mess the molester had made on the floor. She had no idea what to do next. Her heart jumped when the bell on the door rang, and she looked up in fear he had returned to continue his sexual attack.

Peggy looked up and saw Miss Carolyn enter the store. She was on her way to her waitress job at Strickland's Restaurant located next to the ferry slip. Peggy's voice trembled as she gave the greeting. "Good Afternoon, may I help you with something?"

Miss Carolyn smiled her usual captivating smile. "Good afternoon to you, too, darlin'. You girls are all so pretty. Your mama and daddy sure made some beautiful babies."

Peggy gave a half smile. "Thank you, ma'am."

"You okay, darlin'? You don't have much color to that pretty face. You feelin' sick today? There's a lot goin' round these days."

Peggy wanted to tell her what had just happened, but she did not. "No, ma'am, I'm fine."

Theda opened her dresser drawer and threw Rebecca one of her shirts, then grabbed one for herself. They put on the shirts and went to the front of the house to see who was there. They looked out the window and saw Jason talking to Mr. King. Rebecca took a deep breath. She was glad Mary C. was not the visitor. Theda did not like it when Jason sat down in one of the porch chairs. It was as if something Mr. King said pushed him into the chair. She knew something was wrong. She picked up her shorts off the couch, and put them on, and walked through the front screen door to the porch.

"What's wrong, Mr. King?" John King turned to Theda when she came through the door with her question. His face was cracked with sorrow and sadness. She looked at Jason. His eyes were empty, and he looked like he was mentally gone from the porch. "Jason, you talk to me, right now!"

Jason's eyes focused on Theda when she said his name. His throat was dry, and he wanted to get lost in that dark world of his mind he knew so well. Theda's pretty face kept him from leaving and hiding in that safe and remote place. Jason had never experienced the hold Theda had on him. He found a reason to stay, and she was only fifteen years old.

Mr. King did not want to say the words, but it had to be done. "It's Fabian."

Theda's heart felt like it exploded. Rebecca heard what Mr. King said from the living room, and her breath was taken away as she sat down on the couch. Theda sat down in the porch swing and stared straight ahead. The threesome was silent. Neither Jason nor Mr. King knew what to say to Theda.

Mr. King tried his best. "I don't know all the details, but he died a hero."

Theda had her own thought of her brother being a hero. "He was already a hero. Why did he have to be one again?"

"It was his gift. It's what he was and what he did. If he wasn't being a hero, he wouldn't be Fabian Moore."

CHAPTER EIGHT

Mary C. did not mind taking another hot shower, especially with a man like Jack Jarvis holding the bar of soap. She had forgotten how much she liked taking a shower with a man. Mary C. had already lathered him up all over. Jack was squeaky clean, and it was easy for Mary C. to see his excitement. He had his own built-in towel rack. She did like holding a man in her hands. It was Jack's turn to work over her body with that bar of soap. Mary C. never even thought to look for Hawk in the steam from the hot water. It would have been the perfect setting for Hawk to appear. With Mary C. in the haunted house taking a shower with another man, it was the perfect time for all the stars to be aligned, but Hawk did not show himself. Perhaps he did let go of Mary C. and move on to the other side. Mary C. was much more interested in the living than the dead at that particular moment.

With the noise from the shower and the distance from the front door, plus the sexual moans and groans, Mary C. and Jack Jarvis did not hear the timid knock on the front door of the haunted house. Margie tapped on the big door as if she really did not want anyone to hear her. She prided herself on not being afraid of Mr. King's haunted house, but she thought twice about looking through the glass window of the door. She was sorry she had knocked on the door, but was glad no one answered. If no one saw her perhaps the appearance of the carousel could be attributed to the many strange happenings that seemed to occur on a regular basis at the house. Why would any one suspect that it was her who left it on the porch?

Margie held a blanket under her arm. She looked toward the store and saw Susan watching to see if she was really going to leave it. She placed the blanket on the porch floor and gently unfolded it. The blanket fell open, revealing the magic carousel Margie had smuggled back from their trip to the Giant's Motel. Mary C. took it back to Gibsonton, and then Margie brought it back to Mayport. She placed the beautiful antique music box in one of the chairs on the porch. She did not want to leave it on the floor just in case someone did not see it and accidentally stepped on it. Margie looked around one more time to be sure no one was watching her and ran to the store. Mary C. and Jack Jarvis went straight from the shower to Mary C's bedroom to continue her "Let's get better acquainted" Mojo ritual.

Margie walked into the store to relieve Peggy. Miss Carolyn was leaving as she walked in. "Here's another one of the family beauties. Margie, ain't it?"

"Yes, ma'am. How are you, Miss Carolyn?"

"I'm a better person for seeing you two today, that's for sure. You girls have a way of lifting the spirits of another, and you don't even know ya did it. What a wonderful quality to possess. I gotta get to work, or Mr. Willie will be firin' me." She left the store.

As soon as Margie looked into Peggy's empty and sad eyes, she knew something was wrong with her sister. "Good lord, Peggy, you look awful. Are you sick? Why didn't you tell me you were sick?" Peggy surprised Margie when she hugged her and began to cry.

Rebecca Coolie walked out onto the front porch to sit with Theda Moore. She walked past Mr. King and nodded. She wore a long shirt over her panties, with her legs visible from six inches above her knees down to her bare toes. It was more than obvious she was braless under the shirt as her huge rock hard breasts moved slightly as she walked. Mr. King knew he was looking at a young woman with an incredible body. Both men watched her until she sat down next to Theda. She put her arm around Theda's shoulder and pulled her close to her body. Theda responded and leaned to her. Jason wanted them to kiss again, but he kept that thought to himself. Rebecca looked at Jason and talked like they were all family.

"Don't worry, Theda. Me and Jason'll take care of you and Sammy."

Mr. King looked at Jason as to say *You lucky son of a bitch,* but that was just another improper thought he shook from his head. Mr. King knew he could do nothing to comfort Theda Moore.

"I'm gonna go on back to the house now, Theda. I know you're in good hands here, but if you need anything don't hesitate to ask. I'll try to take care of as much as a can, but I know a family member will have to be involved. Try to rest tonight, and I'll come by in the morning once I get things goin'." He looked at Jason. "Why don't you stay with Theda tonight? Your mama will probably be out this way before too long. I know she wants to see Theda and tell her what happened." He looked at Rebecca Moore. He wanted to ask her about Miss Stark's necklace, but knew he needed to leave that business to Mary C. "I'd just stay put young lady, if I was you."

If the ghosts in Mr. King's house came out before dark, they were running wild on that particular day before the sun set. Mary C. was putting on a sexual show for Jack Jarvis and any spirit from this side or other side that might be passing through. It was her way of compartmentalizing Fabian's death. She was an expert at channeling her energy, good or bad, in another direction and getting lost in physical and sexual activity. It was another one of her many gifts. Jack Jarvis thought it was all for him, but it was really for her.

Margie has listened to Peggy describe every moment of her nauseating ordeal. She wanted to comfort her sister but had no idea how to do so. "We have to tell Mother and the police. He just can't do that and then just walk on down the road like nothing happened.

Peggy was afraid. "What if he comes back before they find him? He'll know I told. I'm scared, Margie. What if he lies, and they don't believe me?"

"What do you want me to do?"

"I'll go home and get a bath. I feel real nasty. I need to think about what to do. I don't think it's something that easy to solve. My word against his seems pretty weak to me."

"It's your word against a stranger's; they'll believe you, Peggy."

"The people we know will, but what about the police? I don't know, but you can't tell until I decide what to do. Promise me."

Margie shook her head and hugged her sister. "I promise."

Sofia, Susan and Miss Margaret had the table set in the dinning room with a meal fit for a king, banana pudding and all. They were waiting for Jason to join them for dinner and pick up Billy. Jason did not have the opportunity to tell his mother or anyone else about the invitation for dinner at Miss Margaret's table. And if he did have the opportunity, he would not have mentioned it, because he had forgotten anyway. Miss Margaret smiled at her youngest.

"Sofia, stop looking out the window. Jason will be here when he gets here. Maybe something happened, and he'll just be late."

Sofia plopped down on the couch as frustration took her. Miss Margaret shook her head and walked to check on Billy. She was hoping Sofia would grow out of her feelings for Jason. Miss Margaret knew he was the kind of man who would only bring her sorrow and heartbreak. Sofia jumped up when she heard a car engine. Her heart fell into her stomach when the green family station wagon pulled up to the front porch. Peggy was home for dinner. She had left Margie at the store for the evening shift.

Mr. King drove his 1957 Chevy past the ferry slip. He saw the drifter standing on the bulkhead looking down at the river shore. It was low tide, so about thirty feet of shoreline was visible. The stranger was watching an army of fiddler crabs run in and out of their holes on the river mud. Mr. King slowed the car down and rolled slowly past the unwelcome drifter. The man did not turn as the car went by.

Sofia was disappointed it was her sister, Peggy, walking through the front door. Miss Margaret smiled. "Busy at the store?"

"No, ma'am; real slow."

"You alright, Peggy?"

"I'm not feeling very good. I'm going to take a long hot bath and lie down, if that's okay."

"Of course, it is, dear. Can I get you something?"

"No, ma'am." Miss Margaret watched her daughter walk up the stairs to her room.

Mr. King got out of his car and walked up the steps to the porch of his haunted house. The first thing he noticed was the music box. *What the hell!* For some reason he looked around before he picked it up. He whispered out loud. "Norman, you there?" There was no answer. "Norman, did you do this?" Still nothing. Mr. King picked up the beautiful antique and went into the house. He went straight up to put the carousel in his bedroom. He knew Mary C. would not like it being back in the house. He stopped his movement down the long hallway when he heard the noises he knew so well, coming from Mary C.'s bedroom. He knew it was Mary C. at her best. No man could pass that keyhole without dropping to one knee. Not Mr. King, anyway.   His eye was buried against the metal key hole as soon as his knee touched the wooden floor in front of the door. The pure animal pleasure he would feel far outweighed any consequences that may occur from being caught kneeling in the hallway in the *Peeping John* position.

Big Joe Croom stood at the front door of his house. The alcohol he had consumed at the Gasser had rekindled his courage. He had his own key, but before he used it, he knocked to see if his wife would allow him to talk to her. He saw her coming toward the door through the white curtain on the front glass. The door opened and his one true love stood there looking like a totally different woman than he married.

She was still shrouded in her black mourning attire. Her eyes glared at him as if he were a stranger and did not belong there. He could feel his heart with an irregular beat as they faced each other. Big Joe wanted to be stronger and help his wife find her way back to the life they shared before their son was taken from them. He had always been the rock she needed, but the woman standing in front of him had no needs at all. He wondered if she ever really needed him at all or if it was just the way she was supposed to be. He was hoping she would speak first. Big Joe found the courage he knew he always had. They didn't call him Big Joe for nothing. He decided to have the first word.

"I want to come home and be here with you and the boys. You need to stop this thing before it goes too far. You've worn black long enough."

Stella Croom heard what her husband of twenty-five years said. "You've been drinkin'. I see it in your eyes and smell it on your breath."

Joe nodded. "I've been drinkin', but I know what I'm sayin'. I still want to come home and us be a normal family again."

"Is she dead?" Her question surprised Big Joe. It made her sound crazy, and he didn't like it at all.

"Of course, she's not dead. Stop talkin' like this. You sound like a crazy woman, Stella. You're scarin' me, and I want it stopped. We got three sons to raise into men together, and their mama can't be a crazy woman."

"Why don't we make sure they grow up, so Mary C. can feed 'em to another one of her devil dogs? I'm sure she'll have another beast at her side when she needs one. The devil protects his followers." She slammed the door in Big Joe's face, and he heard the click of the dead bolt lock. He saw her walk away through the white curtain. Big Joe was not leaving again. The sting of the whiskey kept him at the door.

Big Joe heard something behind him. He turned quickly and found himself face to face with the drifter. "I didn't mean to scare ya, sir. Didn't want that at all."

Big Joe's heart was racing from his unsuccessful meeting with Stella, and now a stranger was a few feet away. Big Joe took a defensive stance. "What do want here, mister?"

"I don't mean no harm, sir. I'm just lookin' for work, so I can get across the ferry and get back home to Yulee."

Big Joe did not like the stranger standing in his yard. "There ain't no work. Now, go on."

The drifter smiled. "Go on?"

Big Joe's nostrils flared. "That's what I said, mister, and I didn't stutter when I said it."

"No, ya didn't, friend. It was pretty damn clear." Stella opened the front door and stepped out onto the porch. Big Joe and the drifter looked at her. Joe took a deep breath.

"Go on back in the house, Stella." Big Joe's face went red when the stranger smiled at Stella.

"Don't go back in my account, Stella. This town's got the prettiest women I've ever seen in one place."

Big Joe stepped toward the forward intruder. "I asked you to move on, mister."

The drifter smiled and shook his head. "No, now, that ain't exactly true, sir. You told me to 'go on,' and that ain't really askin' me to move on, now is it? There's a big difference in the presentation of the request. I hope ya can see it from my point of view."

Big Joe was not sure what he was going to do to get the man to leave his property. He turned to Stella. "Get back in the house." She went in and closed the door.

The drifter nodded as she closed the door. "Good night, Stella."

Big Joe had tolerated enough from the disrespectful stranger. The alcohol and the fact that Stella was watching gave him the courage he needed. He threw a big right hand and hit the man flush on the bridge of his nose. Blood exploded from the man's face as he fell to the ground. Big Joe had no intentions of allowing the man to get up off the ground. He began kicking him until he was unconscious and motionless. Big Joe had taken all his mental frustrations out on the drifter. Big Joe took his limp body and threw him in the back of the truck. Stella watched out the front window of the house as the truck drove away. She had sent her three sons to spend the day with her sister, and she was alone.

Big Joe stopped his truck near the sand hill. He looked up at the huge oak tree as he opened the tail gate of his truck. He grabbed the stranger and pulled him out of the back bed of the truck. The man moaned when his body fell the four feet from the truck tail gate to the white sand of the sand hill. He rolled over onto his back. A chill went through Big Joe when he heard the man's voice whisper.

"Didn't mean to make ya mad, mister. I just like pretty ladies. Can't help it. I'll give ya five dollars if you let me kiss her." Big Joe kicked the man in the head, and he quit whispering.

Stella Croom looked out her front window and saw the truck returning. She walked to the door but did not open it. She was prepared to talk to her husband again but through the door. Big Joe was not going to do such a thing ever again. With one angry kick of his number sixteen boot, the wood around the lock shattered and the door swung open. Stella Croom's eyes widened when she saw her husband coming through the door. Big Joe Croom was back home for good.

The drifter tried to stand at the foot of the sand hill. His blood soaked face was coated with the white sand. He staggered and fell back onto the sand and sat there.

Stella Croom was mentally strong, but she was not physically strong enough to fight off Big Joe's sexual drive to be with her. The liquor, the confrontation with the stranger, and his mental state after being away from her created his new level of aggression.   Stella was surprised when he pushed her into the bedroom and locked the door.   She tried not to show her fear, but she knew she could not stop him when he ripped off her black dress and shawl. Her bra and panties were torn away from her body with two strong pulls.   He had never actually thrown her into the bed, but there is a first for everything.   She had always loved the way he looked at her body, and his eyes had not changed.   Stella knew she would have no choice in what was to come. She watched him for the ten seconds it took him to undress. He jumped into the bed like he was not human. When he reached his hand down and touched her between her legs, he felt her excitement, and he knew he would not have to force her to spread her legs. He had already had the first word, and he was planning on having the last.   They would not talk about the drifter.

Margie kept looking out the store window in case the drifter came that way. She would lock the door if she saw him. Peggy was sitting in a deep bath tub filled with hot water. She took a bar of soap and rubbed her private area to clean away the drifter's nasty touch. As she lathered up her tender area, her nipples hardened and she used her fingers to pleasure herself. She moaned a low deep throat sound as her flat stomach muscles contracted, and she released her sexual fluids into the hot water.

Mr. John King moved away from his peep hole when he realized Mary C.'s sexual performance had ended for the time being. He hurried to his room carrying the carousel with him. He wasn't sure what he was going to do with the music box, but the thought of opening that door to the other side again was very enticing. He would consider his options at a later time. Mr. King knew Mary C. and her friend would not leave the room quickly, so he left the carousel and moved quietly down the hall and back downstairs. He would pretend he had been downstairs when Mary C. finally emerged from upstairs.

Rebecca closed Theda's bedroom door. Theda had taken one of Fabian's sleeping pills hoping when she awakened it would all be a horrible dream. Little Sammy was asleep until his normal wake up time of between five and six in the morning. Rebecca stepped into the living room where Jason was sitting on the couch.

"The rest will do her good. We could all use some sleep." Jason did not respond. "You know, Fabian really liked me. He wanted me to stay here with him and Theda. He said he was crazy about me."

"If he said that, he was. Fabian didn't say things he didn't mean." Jason was easy to like. She moved to the couch to be closer. "Would you think I was awful if I asked you to go to bed with just me this time?"

"Not at all. I'm crazy about ya, too."

Mr. King was sitting in the same chair where Mary C. had sat across Jack Jarvis earlier that day. It was also the chair where Margie and Jason had performed the anal connection and discolored the doily. He heard Mary C. coming down the stairs. He saw that the white doily was missing again, but found it when he looked on the floor next to the chair. Mary C. entered the room. He was placing the doily on the arm of the chair.

"I thought I lost the doily again, but it was on the floor. I guess Norman's playin' with my mind again."

Mary C. smiled. "I'm sure that's it, John. I told Jack he could look through some of those bags of clothes in that closet. We're goin' out to Bill's Hideaway for dinner. You wanna go?"

"No, I don't think so. I'm a little spent from all this. I'm gonna stay here with friends that can't die. I need to make a list of things to do to make the funeral arrangements and help Theda all I can."

"You're a strange bird, John, but I sure do like ya." John was pleased by her rare and double-sided compliment. "Did ya tell that girl to stay put?"

"I told her. Jason's gonna stay with them tonight. Theda shouldn't be alone out there. No tellin' what she'll do when this thing really hits her."

"Jason's out there with the Coolie girl?"

Mr. King nodded. "You want me to go get Theda to stay here tonight?"

"I'm gonna go have dinner with Jack. We'll ride out there and see what's goin' on later."

Mr. King smiled and nodded to Jack Jarvis as the two sex birds walked toward the front door. Mary C. looked back at Mr. King. "I don't know how your knees can take that hard wood floor in the hall. Good night, John."

Mr. King remained in his living room as he heard Mary C. start the monster engine of her red Corvette. It roared like a lion when she pressed down the gas pedal to warm it up, and then the car purred like a kitten as Mary C. took her foot off of the gas. Mary C. had a craving for speed. It was another way for her to clear her head. Jack Jarvis had no idea how much his new friend enjoyed a fast ride. He would know in a matter of minutes. As Mary C. drove past Mr. Leek's dock, the drifter stepped out into the road, and she had to slow down so she would not hit him with her car. She drove slowly toward him as he stood there in the road. She stopped next to him.

"The middle of the road ain't the best place to stand, mister." She looked at his battered face. "Damn, mister, you look like you already got hit out here."

He looked at Mary C. "Another pretty woman. This town is the best." He looked at Jack Jarvis. "Nice to see you again, sir. As you can see, not everybody wants to give me a hand. I guess I asked the wrong man for work."

Jack Jarvis did not like the feeling he had as he looked at the stranger. "With that money, I thought you had gone across the ferry by now."

"I kinda like the looks of this town." He grinned and looked down at Mary C.'s legs. Before he could make another comment, Mary C. pushed down the gas pedal and drove away, leaving him standing in the street. She looked into the rearview mirror and saw him still standing in the road.

"If he's still around when we get back, we'll be sure he gets on the ferry. I hope he ain't no fire bug. He smelled like rotten, boiled shrimp."

Mary C. drove at a normal safe speed until she reached the Little Jetties. She knew the history on that deadly curve. Her respect for the short stretch of road was obvious to Jack Jarvis as they rolled through the high-banked turn. It was a different story when the road ahead of them was a straight shot from the Little Jetties to the turn onto Mayport Road. Jack's heart jumped in his granite chest at the same time the Corvette roared and grabbed the road. They were moving at eighty miles an hour in a matter of seconds, with the speedometer on a steady climb. Before the car reached one hundred miles an hour, Mary C. had to slow the machine down to take the turn onto Mayport Road. Jack knew if it was up to Mary C., the race was not over. He never thought he would be so glad to see a police patrol car, but he welcomed the sight of one sitting on the side of Mayport Road as Mary C. turned the Corvette north toward Seminole Road, the way to the Atlantic Ocean. Their ride to the beach was not as dangerous, but Mary C. did spin the car tires a few times on the beach sand as they approached Bill's Hideaway. Jack was able to handle that.

Miss Margaret and two of her daughters, Sofia and Susan, enjoyed the special dinner and Sofia's banana pudding. Peggy did not join them. Sofia's silence announced her disappointment to the others. They would save Margie her share. Sofia was glad her oldest sister was not with them. Margie would just tell her how Jason had always disappointed her, so why would she think this time would be any different. At least Susan did not comment on her obvious sadness. Miss Margaret had to speak her mind.

"I'm worried that something has happened. It's not like Jason to leave Billy for so long or Mary C. for that matter. Why don't you girls take a ride over to Mr. King's and see if every thing's okay. I'll give Billy his bath and get him ready for bed. Just tell them I was worried." Miss Margaret had to smile as her two daughters scrambled to leave the table and go out the front door. "When y'all get back these dishes will be waiting for you!" The green family station wagon was on its way to John King's haunted house.

Theda and her baby, Sammy, were out for the night. Jason and Rebecca were fused together like someone had used a welding torch between their bodies. Jason knew he had never touched a body like hers. She was hard, strong, and aggressive. When it was time to be rough she responded. When Jason took the lead, she followed. When she took the lead, Jason bathed in the attention. Nothing was off limits. She would do anything and everything Jason wanted.

It was the first time in years Stella Croom and her husband, Joe, had indulged in sexual relations before nightfall. She had allowed him to do his will, but the excitement of being taken by a hint of force made her blood boil to its limits. She did not even mind the smell of whiskey, because Joe did no kissing as he took her. It was over, and Joe lay beside her, sleeping from the effects of the alcohol and the sexual peek he reached. Stella had forgotten what pure animal sex was like, but if she were to sleep with Joe, she wanted the sex to be that way all the time. The burning between her legs was almost as strong as the burning in her black heart. She would use her husband's sex drive and desire for her to rid Mayport of the evil Mary C.

Mary C. and Jack Jarvis sat at a corner table in Bill's Hideaway, the ultimate Honky Tonk built up on stilts near the jetty rocks at the mouth of the St. Johns River. The owner, Bill, walked over to their table.

"I can't believe you've come to see us, Mary C. I was worried about you."

"Don't you know by now you can't get rid of me? How are ya, Bill?"

"I'm good, and I'm better now. It's great to see ya. I owe you a dinner. Please let me pay off that debt tonight. It would be my pleasure."

"You don't ever owe me nothing, Bill."

"Please."

She looked at Jack Jarvis who was smiling at the attention she was getting. "Bill, this is my friend, Jack Jarvis."

Bill offered his hand. "Pleased to meet ya, Mr. Jarvis."

Jack took Bill's hand for the manly shake they both expected. "Please call me Jack."

Bill looked at Mary C. as the two men released their hands. "Leave it to you to bring *the* Jack Jarvis into my establishment." He looked back at Jack. "Your reputation precedes you, sir. I heard you just won a great fight with the odds greatly against you. I also heard there was a great commotion out on Black Hammock Island after your fight. Were you still there for the other fireworks, or had you left before all the excitement?"

Mary C. and Jack looked at each other with amazement at the information Bill had become privy to in such a short amount of time. Mary C. had to ask a question before Jack answered Bill's question.

"How in the hell do you know all that crap?"

"I got one of them eyes like Aunt Matilda and Zulmary. I see things before and after they happen." Mary C. shook her head at Bill's little joke that did not make much sense.

"Bill, it's just before things happen, not after things happen. We all know things after they happen."

"Well, I got the sight no matter when it is." He smiled. "And the fact about twenty customers came in after the fight and told me what they saw out there." He looked at Jack. "They thought there was a big fire at one of the buildings, but they weren't sure. There was gun play, too. That's all they knew. They said they high tailed it out of there as soon as they could. Did ya see any of that stuff?"

Jack Jarvis shook his head. "That all must have happened after I left. I don't stay long after I fight. Sometimes when folks get drunk, it gets ugly when they realize they lost their money because of me. I don't hang around too long." He looked at Mary C. "I do stay long enough to sign a few young ladies' bare bottoms, but that's about it." Mary C. had to smile. She did like Mr. Jack Jarvis.

Jason watched the back of Rebecca's head move up and down as she sucked on him as hard as she could. He had held off the explosion as long as he could but she was sucking his juices from down in his toes. She prepared herself for the climax she was working to accomplish. Rebecca was going to be sure she did not let go and took all he could give. She felt Jason's body tense as he tried not to release his hot flow. Rebecca took one last draw and it was too much for Jason to handle. She moaned when the thick hot liquid hit the roof of her mouth and the deep back of her throat. She did not gag or choke as she held her mouth firm around him.

Jason was weak as Rebecca held him tight with her lips. His organ was sensitive to the touch, and he had to pull away and make Rebecca let go. His head cleared and an idea flew through his mind. Jason did not mean to, but he thought out loud. "Oh no, I forgot about the banana puddin'."

Mr. King was sitting on his front porch thinking about using the carousel and his friend Ana Kara, the belly dancer. He was trying not to think about Anna Jo Hamilton, but her face kept flashing in his head. His thoughts of the Wiccan beauty from his past were interrupted when he saw the green family station wagon roll into his front yard. He could see Susan at the wheel, but he was not able to see which other of the sisters were in the car with her. She stopped the car and rolled down the driver's side window. John smiled and made the first greeting.

"Well, hello, Susan. Come on up and set a spell. It's nice on the porch as the night moves in."

"That's alright, Mr. King. I'm fine right here."

The passenger's side door opened, and Sofia stood up looking over the top of the car. "Mother sent us to see if Jason and Miss Mary C. were alright. Jason was supposed to come for dinner and get Billy, but he didn't come. You and Miss Mary C. were invited, too."

Mr. King stood up from his chair. "I wish I had known that. I'm sure my leftovers didn't hold a candle to what you ladies served up at your house. Sorry I missed it."

Sofia was dramatic and anxious. Her eyes were opened as wide as they could be. "Are they alright, Mr. King? Mother's very worried. She had a bad feeling."

"Jason and Mary C. are fine. We did have some bad news, and I'm sure that's why Jason didn't tell us about the dinner and why he didn't show up." The three sisters were all ears after Mr. King "bad news" comment. "Fabian Moore got killed today. We've had to deal with that."

Mary C. and Jack Jarvis had checked into the Sand Piper Hotel on the ocean in Jacksonville Beach, for their own all-night sex rodeo. Before they got settled in the room, Mary C. took Jack skinny dipping in the huge hotel swimming pool known for its icy cold water. It took them both a few minutes for their bodies to adjust to the cold water, but after they did the sexual friction seemed to warm the water surrounding them. Jack Jarvis had never seen anybody like Mary C. He had been hooked, reeled in and landed like a Mule Snapper on the deck of the party fishing boat, Wynema.

Darkness would take Mayport in a matter of minutes. John King sat in his bedroom looking at the carousel music box. He was hoping his resident ghosts would help him decide what to do. He also thought about Mary C.'s theory that the box would not reveal the door to the other side to someone who had not violently taken the life of another human being. John King would not kill someone just to be able to open the doorway. Perhaps her theory had no merit, and if he used the box alone with only thoughts of the door, it would open for him, with Norman leading the way.

He wished Anna Jo was there with him. He usually wished for Ana Kara the belly dancer, but Mary C. had ignited an old flame, and he did not care if Anna Jo Hamilton was a witch or not. She would know what to do. He thought about using the box to find her and bring her to him in a dream. He could have the sex he desired in the dream without her turning him into a frog or something. When he woke up it would be guilt free, because it was only a dream. John King smiled at his silly but desired fantasy.

The sleeping pills had forced Theda Moore into a deep and dreamless sleep. She had no idea Jason and Rebecca were having unbridled, uninhibited and unbelievable sexual relations that would last until they both passed out before morning.

Sofia went to bed right after they told Miss Margaret about the horrible news. She was sad, mad and disappointed. She touched herself for about a half hour and thought of Jason. It was going to be a restless night for the ice-blue-eyed beauty.

The one lone, injured fighting rooster left behind was crowing that it was morning on Black Hammock Island. A caravan of eight police cars stirred up the dirt on the single road leading to the island of thieves, degradation and despair. Each police officer was fully armed and prepared to do battle. They drove right through the broken main gate and onto the island with no interference, resistance or gun play.

When they reached the main house, the cars fanned out in different directions to cover the entire area. Officer Boos stopped his patrol car in front of what was left of the main house and got out to assess the situation. The house had burned completely to the ground. Even the red brick chimney had crumbled from the intense heat of the gas fire. There were a few dead dogs on the ground that had been put out of their misery after being injured in the fights. No one had taken the time to bury them in the mass animal grave located in the woods near the gambling Shed. Big black buzzards were circling in the air, but the smell of smoke and charred wood kept them from landing. Twenty armed police officers had arrived at Black Hammock Island. Each officer had his gun drawn and in the ready-to-fire position. The area looked deserted.

David Boos was in charge. "Check all the buildings and the warehouse over there." He pointed to the building he knew had the stolen goods inside. Paul Short led the way to the six little square buildings where the women were used as sex slaves and held against their will. Five of the buildings were empty, but blood stains and the awful odor in each one told the perverted story of what went on in each one. When he entered the sixth building, his heart dropped into his stomach. He found a young teenage girl still tied to a bed. No one had taken the time to free her from her chains when the exodus from the island began. Paul Short knew finding and saving that child was worth all they had gone through. He knew if Mary C. did kill Aunt Annie, it was one of her better kills. He did not want to think like that, but he couldn't help it. He carried the girl to one of the police cars, and she was taken to St. Luke's Hospital in Jacksonville.

The other buildings were empty. No people, no stolen goods, no vehicles, nothing. Black Hammock Island had been picked clean by the human buzzards of the world. It was as if no one had ever been there. Black Hammock Island became a ghost town overnight.

Jack Jarvis woke up when he felt Mary C.'s hot lips sucking out what little strength he had left in his body. He looked down, and the white bed sheet covered her completely. He could not see her, but he knew she was there.

Rebecca Coolie was up and out of the bed she shared with Jason the entire night. She held Theda's baby, Sammy, in her arms so Theda could sleep longer than usual. Rebecca knew she had to endear herself to Theda like she had done before. Jason would sleep until someone woke him up.

Stella Croom was lying in her bed on her right side and was allowing Big Joe to enter her in that comfortable position. His moans and grunts told her he was almost finished. When he got close to his climax, he did roll her over onto her stomach so he could pump harder. He loved the fact he had taken back his place as Big Joe Croom. Stella was glad she knew how to make him crazy for her--crazy enough to kill.

Mr. King had not used the carousel during the night, but he was still deep into an early morning dream generated from his earlier thoughts of the witch Anna Jo Hamilton. During the dream she wanted him to see something and beckoned him at every turn, but he was unable to reach her. He was not afraid, because he trusted Anna Jo and did not think she would hurt him, dream or not. She did talk to him one time about being a Dream Walker, and perhaps she was actually walking in his dream at that very moment. When he woke up and had not reached her, he strongly considered using the carousel to see if he would be able to bring her to him at his will. It was an exciting thought. His member was hard, but he did not relieve himself.

Sofia was on morning duty at the store and her thoughts were still of Jason. She wanted to see him. She was sad about Fabian's death, but did not like knowing Jason stayed the night with Theda Moore, the fifteen-year-old mother of one. Sofia's jealousy would have been ten-fold if she knew Rebecca Coolie was also staying at the Moore house.

There was no more for the police officers to do on Black Hammock Island. They would recover no stolen items, find no drugs, arrest no gamblers or culprits; they couldn't even catch the crippled rooster. Officers Boos and Short had to be satisfied the evil lawless island was closed down, with little chance of rising from the ashes. They were happy about finding the young girl, but they were hoping for even more. Paul Short stood next to David Boos as the police cars pulled away and headed down the road leading them off the island.

"I'm sorry Fabian got killed. Even though we know he killed the Coolies, he was one hell of a man to have around." David Boos nodded in agreement as Paul had more to say. "You do realize we don't really know if Aunt Annie's dead or not. They were yellin' that she got killed, but I didn't see her. If Mary C. killed her, who's gonna say it? The only thing we know is Fabian got shot by the guards; we think we killed the two guards. That's it. We're the witnesses, and we did the majority of the killin'."

David Boos wrinkled his forehead. "It's all givin' me a headache."

The two policemen would never know about the guard at the back steps Fabian killed. They had no idea Fabian slit Luther Rude's throat the night before in the room with Mary C. The fact that Mary C. killed Aunt Annie would be suspected, but not that she also killed Ida Gold. It would take a little longer than usual for the buzzards to pick Julius Thurber's huge body clean, but they would eventually finish the job. The bright sun reflecting off the white sand would cause an accelerated deterioration of his body. He was gone for good this time.

The guard at the gate when Fabian returned to the island died at the hospital, as did Virgil Grave Digger Hartley from the blow to his Adam's apple. Nine individuals, including Fabian Moore, had lost their lives during the last twenty-four hours of Fight Week on Black Hammock Island. Mary C. was ordering two giant corn dogs for her and Jack Jarvis from Pee Wee's on the boardwalk in Jacksonville Beach. She turned back to Jack. "You want mustard?"

CHAPTER NINE

Rebecca Coolie looked out of the front room window of Theda Moore's house every time she heard a noise. She was concerned about Mary C. coming for their talk. She really wanted to stay with Theda and have the comfort of a beautiful home and a man like Fabian to take care of her. She wanted being clean and comfortable to be an everyday thing. She wasn't sure she could win Jason's affection like she had won Fabian's. She could tell Jason was different when it came to giving his feelings away. The danger, sex and death seemed to just bounce off of him as if he was always prepared for the worst. She felt his dark side and knew he could and would forget her in a matter of minutes, if not seconds. He would always be with his mother and follow her direction and lead. Rebecca remembered the look on his face when he was in the bedroom at Aunt Annie's and he held the big knife in his hand. He would have cut her into tiny pieces to find his mother. She had not thought of that while they were having the night full of sex. She had sexual relations with the man who killed her father and two brothers. She had sex with a former serial killer, her aunt's two lesbian lovers and her aunt. Now, she had just finished a night of more sex with a man who only one day before threatened to kill her with a hunting knife.

Rebecca Coolie knew her eighteen years of life had been insane to say the least. She did not feel she was actually insane herself, but she knew she had dark and sad moments--dark enough to seriously contemplate killing herself. Rebecca also knew the tormentors who drove her to the edge of suicide were gone and would not hurt her again. Her mind was racing with thoughts and questions: *How could she change what she had become? Would the people she met in the future allow her to change?* There were things she did not want to change. She liked the way men looked at her and her sexual knowledge. *Could the necklace be the answer? If Mary C. wanted it so badly, it must be worth a great deal. Something like that could change a person's life, their identity, their present, past, and their future.* Theda's voice broke Rebecca's thoughts of a new life.

"What time is it? I've got to nurse Sammy. Oh, my head." She touched her forehead with her hand. She looked at the clock on the wall. "Oh, my God, it's almost noon. Why didn't you wake me up?"

Rebecca lied. "I tried, but you were out in there. I took care of Sammy, but I'm sure he's pretty hungry by now." Theda did not say anything else. She went to nurse her baby.

The red Corvette was headed back to Mayport. Jack Jarvis was at the wheel while Mary C. sat in the passenger's seat with her bare feet on the dash. She was actually moving her toes to the beat of the song, "Splish Splash" by Bobby Darin. Jack could hardly keep his eyes on the road with Mary C.'s calf muscles bulging and flexing as she continued her foot dance on the dash board.

Theda Moore heard a truck engine in the front yard and stepped into the living room to look out the front window. Sammy was hooked to one of her milk filled breast. She smiled at the sight of Rebecca Coolie leaving in her truck. She was running again and Theda couldn't have been happier. She made sure the front door was locked and went to the room where Jason was sleeping. She lay next to him and continued nursing her child.

Mary C. changed her foot tapping cadence on the dash board when "Splish Splash" ended and the sound of the Platters and their big hit, "The Great Pretender," softly filled the car. Mary C. wished she was slow dancing with Jack Jarvis. She looked away from the front windshield and was admiring Jack's profile. She did not see the truck pass them going in the opposite direction. The high speed of the truck made Mary C. take a second look. It only took an instant for Mary C. to realize the truck belonged to Rebecca Coolie. She had no doubt the Coolie girl was on the run again.

"Stop the car, Jack!"

Jason woke up at twelve-thirty to the aroma of a pot roast stew cooking. The pleasant smell had traveled down the hall. He walked to the kitchen and saw Theda at the stove.

"Wow, that really smells good! What time is it, anyway?"

"About twelve-thirty. You were sleepin' so hard, I didn't have the heart to wake you. I'll cook you some breakfast if you'd like something."

"How 'bout some toast and coffee. I feel like dunkin'."

Theda smiled. "Me too. That sounds great."

"You dunk, too?"

"Always have."

Jason looked down the hall. Theda knew what he was thinking. "She was gone when I got up. I guess she was afraid to face your mama. I know I'd be. You think she's got that necklace?"

"It don't matter what I think. Mama thinks she does, and if she's gone again, no tellin' what mama will do if she finds her. I sure hope she comes back."

Theda's smile left her face. "For ya mama, or for you?"

Jason smiled and stepped to Theda. The kiss was even better than the other one. Jason turned Theda around and leaned her over the kitchen table. He lifted her bath robe exposing her bare butt. It was time for Theda to scream with pleasure again. The toast and coffee would have to wait. Jason was dunking more than his toast.

Jack Jarvis was behind the wheel of the red Corvette as Mary C. directed him in the skills of a high-speed pursuit. "There's no possible way she'll out run this car. We'll catch her before she gets to the end of the road."

Jack was watching the road as he hit eighty miles an hour. "I don't usually drive this fast. I don't want to kill us. Don't forget the cop from yesterday. That could be his spot for the week, ya know."

Mary C. did not care about anything except Rebecca Coolie. "Run that whore dog down. I've had enough of this. I gave her too long to think about it. What's wrong with me anyway?" She looked at Jack Jarvis as he tried to keep the car on the road. "You're what's wrong with me, Jack." He took his eyes off of the road and looked at her as if to say, *What the hell are you talking about?*

The right tire of the car went off the asphalt and hit the gravel shoulder of the road. When Jack tried to pull the car back onto the hard road the sharp turn of the wheel buried the right front tire into the loose gravel. The high speed and the lower tire caused the car to spin in a circle and flip into the ditch next to the road. As the car began to turn over, Mary C. knew she was thrown out of the car and into the air. She braced herself for the hard landing. The ditch was full of water and mud, and even though her landing was still hard, she knew it did not kill her. The car flipped over twice before it stopped upside down. Mary C. lay on her stomach in the mud. She lifted her head to find Jack Jarvis. At that moment she had no idea the steering wheel had locked his legs in the car and on the second complete flip his neck was broken in the same manner Steve Crane Robertson had died at the curve of the Little Jetties. Jack Jarvis would be the tenth death to occur with Mary C. in close proximity. The death count was now into double figures.

Rebecca Coolie was at the end of Mayport Road. She had seen Mary C. in the red Corvette and was looking back to see if she was being pursued by her brief ex-partner and bitter enemy. Her decision was to either turn left on Atlantic Boulevard or turn right to go into the city. Her options for hiding places were limited if she turned left, so she headed west to see what the city of Jacksonville might have to offer.

Two cars stopped to help Mary C. She knew the man who was standing above her in the ditch. He was one of the Mayport shrimpers, David Pack. He moved his three-hundred-pound body down into the ditch. "Miss Mary C., you alright?" He took her extended hand.

"I think so, David. I don't feel like I broke nothin'."

"Maybe you just need to stay put and let us get an ambulance. Sometimes folks don't know when they're hurt." Mary C. and David looked toward the noise of the Corvette being turned over by three other men who had stopped to help. When the car fell upright, Jack Jarvis was still in the driver's seat. Mary C. knew by the way he looked, the Jackal was gone. Rebecca Coolie was gone, too.

Paul Short and David Boos had caught the ferry back to Mayport after their useless raid on Black Hammock Island. They wanted to talk to Mary C. and Jack Jarvis to see if they could get any information about what happened on the island before the gun battle erupted. They both knew their chances of getting anything out of Mary C. were slim to none, but perhaps Mr. Jarvis would cooperate. They pulled up in front of Mr. King's house, and both officers got out when they saw Mr. King sitting on the porch.

Mr. King had been making arrangements for Fabian's funeral most of the morning. He remained seated as the officers approached him. "Afternoon, gentlemen."

Paul Short nodded his greeting. "Mr. King, Mary C. wouldn't be close by would she?"

"Ain't seen her since late yesterday afternoon."

Sofia walked out of the store and looked toward Mr. King's house hoping to see Jason. She saw the police car driving away, and Mr. King waved at her. She waved back but was disappointed again; no Jason. It was Susan's turn to cover the store. Miss Margaret had brought Susan to the store before she ran some errands, meaning Sofia would have to walk home. Peggy was home still licking her mental wounds and taking care of Billy. Miss Margaret saw Mr. King on the porch and pulled the station wagon next to the house. She rolled down the driver's side window.

"John, the girls told me the awful news about Fabian. Horrible, just horrible. What is goin' on around here? Makes you want to just pack up and get out before one of yours has something awful happen to them."

John nodded. "I've had a sad mornin' tryin' to get things in order for Fabian's funeral and poor Theda."

"You're a good man, John. You know I don't mind, but Billy's been with us almost two full days now, and it just isn't like Jason or Mary C. to go without him that long."

"I got no answer for ya on that, Margaret. You're a good woman." Miss Margaret smiled and drove the station wagon away. Mr. King sat back in his favorite spot, and Sofia started walking home.

Paul Short looked out the front windshield of his patrol car and saw the flashing lights of a fire truck, an ambulance and two other police cars. He also recognized Mary C.'s red Corvette as it was being hooked and pulled by a Big Chief Tire tow truck. Chip Parman was at the wheel and moving away from the scene. David Boos spotted Mary C. talking to a policeman next to the back door of the ambulance. She had wiped some of the mud off of her body, but still looked dirty and battered. They both got out of the car when Paul Short drove up next to the fire truck and stopped. They moved directly to Mary C. She looked up at the two officers as they walked up.

"Late again, boys. I hope y'all arrested Aunt Annie today for all her sinful ways. I was outraged at what went on out there."

Paul Short overlooked her sarcasm. "You alright?"

The policeman standing with Mary C. answered for her. "She's just bruised up pretty bad, but her friend wasn't so lucky."

Paul Short looked at David Boos, and then they both looked at Mary C. David Boos opened the back door of the ambulance. His usual calm stomach went sour when he saw the body of Jack Jarvis on the gurney. He stepped away from the door. Mary C.'s eyes burned another hole in his soul. To think that another real man was taken away in his prime was incomprehensible. He did not want to, but something made him look at Mary C. again. She was still staring into his eyes.

"I ain't gonna buy another red Corvette."

With the thought of pulling out his gun and shooting Mary C. raging in Officer Boos' head, the green family station wagon rolled up next to the accident scene. Mary C. stepped away from the others and walked to the station wagon. Miss Margaret talked out the window.

"Oh, dear God, my child, are you alright?"

"Can you take me home, Miss Margaret?"

Sofia's walk home was slow and full of thought. She heard a car engine coming up behind her, and she stepped off the road to let it pass. It was the sound of Jason's truck. He was, no doubt, going to her house to get Billy. He rolled slowly along side of her as she walked.

"Do you ride with strangers, little lady?"

Sofia's heart ran wild. "Only handsome ones." She was thrilled to play a little game with Jason. He stopped the truck.

"Then jump on in."

Sofia hurried to the passenger's side door and jumped in. 'We were worried about you last night."

"I know, I didn't mean to miss supper with y'all."

She interrupted him. "That's okay. You lost your best friend. You must be so sad."

Jason pushed down the gas pedal and did not respond. Sofia understood, and she would be quiet for a little while. They rode in silence until her house came into view ahead of them on the left. Jason's surprising words were like music to Sofia's ears.

"You wanna go somewhere and get something to eat? I'd like some ice cream from the Dairy Queen." Sofia knew it was a long ride to 3rd Street at Jacksonville Beach, but she was excited.

"That would be nice, if you feel like it." Her heart raced when Jason turned the truck around, and she knew they were leaving Mayport. Miss Margaret drove the family station wagon up to Mr. King's house. He was still sitting on the porch. Mr. King stood up when he saw Mary C., in her condition, step out of the car. He moved off of the porch to assist her.

Oh, my Lord, what happened?"

Miss Margaret answered the question. "She was in an accident. That fast car flipped over and threw her out into the ditch. It's the Lord's will she's not dead."

Mr. King reached the steps holding Mary C.'s arm. "I can make it inside, John. I'm really not hurt that bad, just sore all over. I'm sure I'll feel it even more tomorrow. I'm just gonna lay down and rest now." She reached the top step and turned to face Mr. King. "Jack's dead. Just that quick, John. He's dead." Mr. King could not respond to the new awful news. Mary C. opened the front door and looked at Mr. King again. "John, you think Jack might come stay here with us?"

Mr. King was surprised with her ghostly inquiry, but he had the answer. "He'd sure be welcome here." He turned and looked at Miss Margaret as Mary C. went into the house. Miss Margaret had advice.

"Keep an eye on her, John. She could still be in shock. Sometimes it doesn't show until later. I don't know how much she can take--or any of us, for that matter."

The sound of Jason's truck took their attention from the subject at hand. Jason looked out the side window. He knew something was wrong. Mr. King stepped to the truck as it slowed down.

"Everything's fine, Jason. Your mama was in an accident with the car. She's in the house and she's gonna be okay." Jason was relieved at Mr. King's words. But, his old friend was not finished. "Jack Jarvis was killed. The car rolled over on him."

Sofia looked at Jason. She was glad Mary C. was fine. She was sad a man died. She still wanted to get some ice cream with Jason. The immediate possibility of that happening went out the window when Jason jumped out of the truck and went into the house.

Sofia stepped out of Jason's truck and got into the station wagon with her mother. Miss Margaret was sorry about the accident, but she was glad Sofia was not going off with Jason. They were driving home in silence when they saw the drifter walking past their house. As they rolled up to the front porch, he stopped to watch the women get out of the car. Miss Margaret did not look his way, but Sofia did. He nodded and smiled as she turned her head away and followed her mother into the house. Peggy was watching him from the upstairs window. Her heart raced as he walked away. He did not see Peggy at the window.

Paul Short sat at Mr. Butler's desk at the police station holding the black book about Mary C. He held it up to David Boos. "Do we add the new names or throw this thing in the trash?"

"I don't want to get wrapped up in that book like he was. I think it would be easy to get caught up in something like that."

"There's a lot of wild information in here. Let's just leave it where it was. Who knows? We might need it one day." There was a familiar voice at the office door. The man hater, Debbie Butler, was looking for some new bounty hunters to go find Tom Green. Paul Short opened the middle desk drawer and dropped the black book back where he found it.

Miss Margaret was in the kitchen when Sofia walked out onto the porch and sat in a chair. She actually wanted to will Jason to come to her. She stared down the road and chanted in her head for him to come to her. She felt their attachment was strong enough for him to know her sadness and needs. Sofia knew it was like that before and could be again, even with all the things that had happened to interfere with them being together. The front door opened and Peggy walked out onto the porch. She handed Billy to Sofia.

"Here. You hold him a little while. I gotta get out of here." She walked past Sofia and got into the family station wagon. Sofia watched Peggy drive away. Miss Margaret stepped out onto the porch.

"Peggy's a little antsy today. Said she needed to go somewhere. Hope she's not getting sick."

"I'm sure she's fine, Mother. She never really complains too much, you know."

Miss Margaret smiled at her youngest. "Sofia, you are so smart and kind. How was I blessed with such a daughter?"

Sofia surprised her mother. "Maybe you and daddy went to the tree. Maybe I'm an oak baby."

Miss Margaret took a deep breath and pursed her lips. "And maybe not, little Missy."

Sofia was smiling at her mother's funny reaction to her oak baby comment. The sound of an approaching vehicle took both their attention from the odd but funny conversation.

It was Jason. Sofia just knew she had willed him to come to her. She was happy their love was still as strong as it was before. Miss Margaret was hoping he was only coming for Billy. The truck stopped in front of the house. Jason stepped out and walked to the porch. "Evenin', ladies. How's that boy doin'?"

Miss Margaret knew Sofia would answer. "He's just fine but missing his daddy." She stood up and held Billy up so Jason could take him. Jason took him into his arms.

"Mama said to tell you she's sorry we didn't come sooner, and thank you so much for takin' such good care of Billy."

Miss Margaret gave a half smile. "It was our pleasure. Anytime."

"Mama says she'll feel better if Billy's sleeping next to her tonight." He looked at Sofia. "After I drop Billy off I'd like to go get that ice cream. You still interested in takin' that ride?"

Miss Margaret's heart sank deep down into her stomach as Sofia nodded her beautiful head. It sunk even deeper when Sofia jumped off the porch and headed to the truck. Sofia turned to face her mother as Jason walked with her.

"Be back in a little while, Mother."

Miss Margaret watched the truck roll away. She thought it was odd for a man to go for ice cream after he had just lost his best friend and his mother was in an automobile accident that killed a man. *What was Jason, anyway?*

Mr. John King passed by Mary C.'s room. He did not consider dropping to one knee and looking through the key hole. He had the carousel on his mind and the possibilities of the beautiful antique opening the door to the other side at some time in the near future. Mary C. was not asleep. She thought about Jack Jarvis and the similarities he had with Hawk. She usually did not ponder on it very much, but for once she did wonder why the men she cared for were all ripped away from her when she had such good feelings for them. Mary C. thought about her brother Bobby. He said they both had gifts and curses. They had to learn to live with both sides. She missed that crazy fool of a brother.

There was a knock on her bedroom door. "It's me, mama. Got somebody here wants to see ya."

"It's open." Jason took Billy to his grandmother.

Debbie Butler had placed five thousand dollars in cash on the desk for both lawmen to see. "I'll give you two another one when you say you'll take the job and two more when the job is done."

David Boos shook his head. "We are not bounty hunters, Miss Butler. You asking us to do something we just can't do."

"You do know somebody's gonna do it for the money. I thought I'd give you two one more chance. You know about this Tom Green. You almost got him the last time. This time you will. I just know it."

"The answer is 'no', Miss Butler. Now, please don't come to us with this offer again."

She stood up and took the money off of the desk. "I thought you were my father's friends. If you find the courage or realize it's the right thing to do, call me. I'll wait two days, and then I'll find someone else."

Jason stopped the truck in the parking space in front of the Dairy Queen at Jacksonville Beach. He got out and went to the window to order Sofia's request and a chocolate dipped cone for himself. Sofia wanted a strawberry short cake topped with ice cream and whipped cream. He looked to his left and saw a smiling face he had not seen in some time. It was Older Peggy. She was Sofia's cousin and the sexual instructor for Sofia's sister, Peggy. Peggy was Older Peggy's namesake.

She was standing next to a car. Older Peggy was a full figured woman but not fat. She could wear shorts because her legs were hard with no fat pockets showing. Her breasts were always her main points of attraction, and she wore the low cut shirts to show what the law would allow. Her cleavage line looked like it was a long road leading to bigger and better things. Older Peggy was standing with her roommate and sometimes lover, Betty. It must have been a night for the opposite sex because two Mayport men, Billy Wells and the oldest Steen brother, Carly, seemed to be Peggy and Betty's dates. They all watched Peggy walk over to Jason and give him a kiss on his lips. Sofia looked out the car window as her eyes opened wide. Jason could tell Peggy had been drinking. The kiss ended.

"Jason, Jason, Jason. Where the hell have you been?" She turned back to Betty. "Ain't he the best lookin' thing around?" She did not wait for an answer from her friend. She turned back to Jason. "You threw me off that mountain, boy. I ain't recovered from that yet. Still think about it when I'm alone." She looked into the car. "Is that my beautiful cousin, Sofia, with you? I ain't seen her, either. Come on out here girl and hug my neck."

Sofia was more than happy to leave the restrictions of the truck and join Jason. She was hoping to get between the next kiss. Peggy hugged Sofia and whispered in her ear. "He's a keeper. Don't let him get away." The hug ended. Sofia wasn't sure how she felt. She was jealous at first, but what a nice thing for her cousin to say. Peggy walked over and stood with Billy Wells. "Y'all don't be a stranger. Tell ya mama and sisters I said 'hey'."

Jason handed Sofia her Dairy Queen treat as the car with Peggy in the back seat pulled out of the parking lot. Billy Wells was wrapped around her like a snake. Jason turned and walked back to the truck with Sofia.

Mr. King left the temptation of the carousel in his bedroom and went outside to sit on his front porch to watch the sun drop down on the other side of the St. Johns River. As soon as he sat down in his chair he saw someone in his peripheral vision to his left. When he turned to see who was on the porch, the figure moved around the far corner of the porch out of his line of sight.

Mr. King got up out of his chair and stepped quickly to the far end of the porch. He looked around the corner. "Is that you, Norman? You don't have to run from me. I could use the company. Thanks for finding the doily. I hope it didn't cause you too much trouble with the others."

He saw movement in the bushes behind his house. Mr. King stepped off of the porch and walked toward a group of crape myrtles. His heart jumped when someone ran from behind the thick bushes. Mr. King could not get to the person. They were too far away and shielded by the plants. The unwanted visitor darted out of Mr. King's yard and into the woods behind Miss Margaret's store. He hurried in that direction and stopped when he recognized Stella Croom as the runner. It was her second time coming around. This time she came all the way to the house.

Jason stopped his truck under the Jacksonville Beach Pier. They had eaten their ice cream in the parking lot of the Dairy Queen with more eating than talking. Sofia was ready, willing and able to be alone with Jason and rekindle their true love affair. She moved over in the seat and kissed him passionately the moment he stopped the truck. Jason did not care if they talked or not. He reached under her blouse and touched her breasts one at a time. Sofia continued the kiss while he unsnapped her pants and put his hand down them. His fingers were under her panties and feeling her wetness in a matter of seconds.

Sofia moaned and ended the kiss so she could help pull her pants off. Soon they were on the truck floor as Jason slid from behind the steering wheel and pulled Sofia over his lap. He slid inside her the same way he slid into Theda that morning and the night before. Sofia kissed him with wild noises and pushed her hips down as hard as she could to get Jason deeper. She sucked his tongue as if she wanted to swallow it. That was something new and exciting from Sofia. She stopped the tongue sucking for a moment and whispered in Jason's ear. "I love you. What do you want me to do?"

Mr. King was upstairs walking down the hall to his bedroom. He was walking softly so he would not disturb Mary C. and Billy. He heard Mary C.'s voice. He stopped and listened. She was talking to the baby. "I wish you didn't look so much like your mama, boy. I can't look at you and not think of her. I'll bet it drives your daddy crazy, too."

John knocked on the door. "Mary C., can I come in?"

"It's open, John."

He turned the doorknob and walked into the room. "I didn't want to wake you, but I heard your voice and thought we could talk a minute."

Mary C. was sitting up in the bed with Billy next to her. John could see her bare breasts through her thin night shirt. He would try not to look directly at her nipples. Her face was bruised under her eye. "What's on your mind, John?"

"That bruise came up quick on your face."

"Oh, that happened yesterday on Black Hammock. The ones from the wreck won't show up 'til later."

"I'm sorry about Fabian and now Mr. Jarvis. There's a dark cloud over this town, Mary C. It don't look like it's ever gonna lift."

"You think it's me, John?"

For the first time Mary C. surprised Mr. King. He had no answer for such a question. He only had another question. "What do you think it is, Mary C?"

"I could say it was this haunted house. If ghosts really live here they could be the dark cloud you mentioned. We got burial grounds all around us, some Indian, some Spanish. We've had Voo Doo, devil worshipers, that damn oak tree, magic music boxes, devil dogs and even a witch, who might be comin' back."

Mr. King could not help his thoughts. He liked the idea of Anna Jo Hamilton returning to Mayport.

Mary C. was serious. "None of this is new to Mayport. We've lived here all our lives. You longer than me. It's been a mean and brutal place ever since I can remember. There ain't no special reason for it, nobody to blame. I was just wonderin' if you thought it might be me causin' all this hell on Earth."

"Mary C., I'm your friend, always have been, always will be. I know the truth and reason behind your actions, good or bad. But, you must understand when folks that don't know ya hear about the things you've done, if you had to or not, they're gonna think how strange it is. They're gonna think, *why does it all happen to her?*

Some folks were born for excitement and trouble. You do seem to fit the category. How many coincidences take place before it's not a coincidence any more?"

Mary C. smiled. "Damn, John, how long ya been plannin' that speech? That ain't somethin' ya just made up in a second or two. I got no idea what the hell you just said. Hell, I'm sorry I asked ya. I thought you'd say, 'No, Mary C., it ain't none of it been your fault.' I won't ask that question again. And I got no idea when a coincidence ain't one no more. Jesus, John." Mr. King had to smile at Mary C.'s comment. He knew that particular conversation was over.

Jason opened the door to one of the rooms at the Sea Breeze Motel in Atlantic Beach. Sofia walked in first and he followed. They knew they only had a few hours together, but that would have to be enough for the time being. Sofia hopped in the bed before Jason could lock the door. She was kneeling down on the bed and completely naked when he turned around. She looked tall even on her knees. Her porcelain white skin was in contrast to the other women he had been with. Both Rebecca and Theda had dark and tanned skin. Sofia was a beautiful young woman. Her body was in perfect proportion and her ice blue eyes, full lips and perfect white teeth topped off her sexual appeal. Jason's clothes hit the floor, and he was on top of Sofia like the wild animal he was. She crumbled under him as he took her down to the mattress.

Stella Croom walked into her house. The twins, Chuck and Buck, and her other son, Pee Wee were sitting in the living room playing cards. All three looked up and smiled as she walked past them and went into her bedroom. Stella hurried and took a gun from under her shirt and put it back in the dresser drawer.

Sofia was kneeling down in the motel bed with Jason behind her. He was pumping her harder than ever before. He had always been gentle with Sofia, but her "do anything" attitude had ignited the real animal in Jason. He wanted her that way, but it just never seemed to materialize until that night. She wasn't a screamer like Theda, but Jason was excited when he heard a few new noises of pleasure coming from Sofia.

Mr. King walked into his living room where Mary C. was sitting in a rocking chair with Billy. He had something on his mind and he had waited too long to tell Mary C.

"I shoulda told you when it first happened, but you've had so much on your plate that I just didn't know how to tell ya."

"Holy shit, John, what is it now?"

"Stella Croom's been sneakin' 'round the house. I saw her first starin' at the house from the side of the store. When I went to talk to her she ran off. Then today she was on the porch when you were sleepin', and she ran off before I could catch her. I don't mind her starin' from a distance, but comin' right up on the porch makes it all different."

Mary C. got up out of the rocking chair. The light shone through her shirt revealing the fact she was braless. Mr. King enjoyed the moment. He did not enjoy the other fact that Mary C. handed him the child.

"I'm goin' to see her. Can you handle Billy for a little while? I won't be long."

Mr. King was uncommonly surprised by her actions again. "I didn't mean for you to have to go see her, Mary C. I just thought you should know."

"You're right; I should know, but she should know I ain't gonna stand for her being a threat to me, Jason, or this child. People get crazy and take revenge out on loved ones when they can't get to the one they hate. It would be just like her to try and take Jason or Billy away, so I could feel her pain. That ain't gonna happen. Now, can ya keep Billy or not? Oh, and I need your car."

Peggy drove to the store to be with Margie. She wanted to talk, and Margie was the only one who knew what had happened to her. Margie was glad to have the company.

Mary C. turned off the car lights and stopped Mr. King's 1957 Chevy on a dirt road leading to Stella Croom's house. She surveyed the house for any movement, but it was late and most people were either in bed or preparing to call it a night. The only vehicle in the yard was the blue Falcon Mary C. had given to Joe Croom. Mary C. thought Big Joe was most likely out shrimping. Most of the shrimpers were night shrimping for hoppers. Mary C. drove the Chevy closer to the house, but parked about fifty yards away.

Stella Croom made her three sons go to bed early, just because she was tired of them and she said so. Stella was glad to be alone, again. She had been a sexual plaything and slave to Big Joe for about forty-eight hours, and that was enough for a while. She was hoping he would stay out shrimping for a few days. At least she had a full night without him pawing at her. It would be a perfect evening to walk outside and sit on the steps of her small front porch.

Stella sat down as a cool breeze tickled her bare nipples under her thin night shirt. Her breasts were tender to the touch from Joe's hard sucking and pinching, but it still felt good when her nipples hardened as the cool air touched them. She took a deep breath and thought about her son, Joe. She never heard one sound when Mary C. came out of the dark. Stella Croom only felt the brutal slap of Mary C.'s black jack when it hit her in the back of the head. She fell forward and her face slammed onto the wooden planks of the small porch. The collision with her face and the wood was as damaging as the blow to the back of her head. Stella Croom did not move or make a sound. Mary C. drew her hand back holding the weapon high to deliver the fatal blow to her enemy and new victim. She had second thoughts about completing the killing. Her hesitation was short lived when she thought about Stella recovering and continuing her quest to hurt her or her family. Mary C. did not want to spend her time worrying about when Stella Croom was going to run out of the dark and attack her. The second swing of the black jack delivered the death blow. Mary C. reached down and took Stella's gold wedding band off of her finger and a necklace off of her neck.

Jason left Sofia at her door and drove back to Theda's house. Sofia tiptoed up the stairs to her bedroom. It was past midnight, and the house was quiet and dark. Miss Margaret has watched Sofia get out of Jason's truck and walk up to the porch, but she did not go out to confront her youngest about being out with Jason so late. Sofia stood at her bedroom door and could see a light shining though the bottom space between the door and the floor. She opened the door and looked in. Her eyes widened when she saw her sister, Margie, lying in her bed reading a book. Sofia closed the door.

"What are you doing in here?"

"Waiting on you, what else?"

"Why?"

"I'm jealous. I thought we could talk about it."

"There's nothing to talk about, because I don't believe you're jealous. You're just going to tell me how he's going to hurt me and he'll never be completely mine. Please don't, because I don't care. I think he's going to be mine, but if he isn't, then I'll take on your way of thinking and be with him when I can. Now, if you don't mind, sex with Jason really wears me out. I need to rest just in case he comes around tomorrow."

Margie smiled. She did love Sofia, but her little sister's last comment was far out of her character. She knew Sofia had changed drastically after her brutal ordeal with killing Carlton Steen and sexual rampage with Jason while on their way to the Giant's Motel.

"Well, I guess you're going to be alright after all. I'll stop worrying about you and see if Jason can make me sleep better, too. Good night."

Mary C. stopped Mr. King's 1957 Chevy when she saw the drifter walking on the edge of the road. He was right next to the driver's side window. "You do get around don't ya, mister?"

He held his hands up. "I ain't doin' nothin' wrong ma'am. Just a evenin' stroll."

Mary C. surprised him when she left the car engine running, but got out of the car. He could have reached out and grabbed her like he did Peggy at the store. He looked into Mary C.'s eyes and saw the look he had seen before. He knew she was not your run of the mill scared woman. This one had faced danger and survived to tell about it and face it again. Her voice was confident and did not quiver.

"I don't think you belong here, mister. It's time for you to move on down the line, don't ya think?"

"I was hopin' to last a little longer, ma'am. There's an interestin' storm comin' this way, and I'd like to be here when it hits. This little town is ready for a cleanin'."

"It'll be much cleaner when you're gone."

He nodded. "Can't argue with ya there, little lady."

Mary C. reached into the car window. The drifter stepped back in fear of her pulling out a gun and killing him right on that spot. He was relieved when he saw she had no gun. Mary C. held a ten dollar bill in her hand. She stepped to the man and tucked it into his coat pocket.

"This should get you across the ferry and where you need to go. You look like a gin man to me." Mary C. smelled burnt wood as she stood near the stranger. She knew that odor very well.

The man smiled. "I'm a tad partial to the clear liquors ma'am, but I have been known to drink my full share of the ones with color."

The ferry horn blew as the big car carrier pulled away from the Fort George side and headed to Mayport. "Time for you to catch the ferry."

"Silly me, I thought we was gettin' along so good."

"If you come back, I will make sure you die here."

The man smiled again. "You're a little late for that, but I do believe ya."

Mary C. turned to the car. He was still disrespectful. "I'll give ya ten dollars for a kiss."

She opened the door, got into the car and looked out the driver's side window. "It takes a lot more than ten dollars to get one of my kisses." Mary C. pushed down the gas pedal, and the car started moving away. The man yelled as the car rolled farther away.

"I'll start savin' up."

Jason got into bed with Theda but let her sleep. He would have sexual relations with her in the morning, or earlier if Sammy woke them up in the middle of the night. Theda realized he had returned to stay with her. She smiled and rolled over placing her arm across Jason's chest. A chill ran through Jason's sexually drained body. There was something about Theda Moore.

Mr. King was rocking Billy in the living room when he heard his 1957 Chevy drive up in front of his house. He heard Mary C.'s footsteps on the porch and the door open.

"In here, Mary C. He just fell asleep. He's been good, though. Don't cry much."

Mary C. walked into the room. "Don't cry at all."

"No, I guess he don't. You alright?"

"I'm fine, John." She took the baby out of Mr. King's arms. "I'll take him up to bed. Thanks for takin' care of him. If you're not too tired, I'd like to sit and talk a while."

"I'll make some coffee, if you'd like some."

"I don't need no coffee, but make you some, and I'll be right back down."

Rebecca Coolie drove her truck into the Gator Motor Lodge parking lot. She was fifty miles from Mayport. She reached into the truck's glove compartment and took out her envelope full of money. She felt under the driver's seat and touched the leather bag containing Miss Stark's necklace. Rebecca smiled a tired smile and went into the registration office to get a room for the night.

Mr. King sat on his front porch sipping a late evening cup of coffee when Mary C. walked out the front door and joined him. "You'll be up all night, John, drinkin' that coffee so late."

"You know, it don't bother me none. I can sleep no matter what. What's on your mind?"

"A few things. I know if we go on another day, we won't get a chance to talk with Fabian's funeral and all."

"What is it, Mary C.?"

"Well, one thing is the Coolie girl's gone again. Once Fabian was out of the picture, she took off. She told me she had the necklace. We were gonna make a deal." Mr. King let her continue. "I told you earlier, I wasn't sure how I felt about hearin' that Anna Jo was out at Black Hammock a few weeks ago."

"If it's true, I wonder why she was out there with Annie."

"Annie said Anna Jo went there to tell her about some dreams she was havin' about Annie's evil ways. She was there to save her soul. She also talked to Annie about dreams she had about me. I sure would like to see Anna Jo."

Mr. King saw a moment of caring and friendship in Mary C. It was not like her to show such feelings. He wondered if she realized how she sounded. "You think she might come here to see you?"

"I thought that, but I don't know." She saw the expression on Mr. King's face. "You'd like her to come here wouldn't ya?"

Mr. King smiled. "I'd like to see her again."

Mary C. nodded. "Well, Mr. John King, you don't care if she's a witch or if she's been dead for three years." Mary C. moved her eyebrows up and down. "You want a little bit of Anna Jo Hamilton."

Mr. King smiled an even bigger smile. He could not recall his house guest ever making such a playful gesture. "Ain't that the truth." He wanted to tell Mary C. he could use the carousel to bring Anna Jo to him, but he didn't.

Another brutal day had ended in Mayport. Sofia would toss and turn and think about getting and keeping a hold on Jason. Rebecca Coolie would fall asleep but dream about her day on Black Hammock Island, the sex with Jason, and kissing Theda Moore. There was something about Theda Moore.

Stella Croom's dead body would be found by her son, Pee Wee, when he woke up early and went outside to play on the tire swing. Jason and Theda would have morning sex with her baby lying on a blanket on the floor by the bed.   Mr. King would not use the carousel, but he would dream about Anna Jo Hamilton.   In the dream she wanted to show him something, but when the drifter was also walking in his dream, Mr. King forced himself to wake up. He wasn't prepared to see the stranger, and it scared him. Mary C. slept with Billy next to her.   She did not dream about killing Stella Croom.   Mary C. would have no dreams.   The threat of Stella Croom was gone. Billy and Mary C. both slept like babies.

CHAPTER TEN

The elusive, crippled rooster crowed out a good morning on Black Hammock Island, but no one was there to wake up to his call. The night shrimpers of Mayport were docking and unloading their boats. Mr. Al Leek was waiting on the dock as Joe Croom's boat, *Miss Stella,* floated up slowly next to the pylons. Mr. Leek had a heavy heart as the carrier of sad and life-changing news. Big Joe threw the thick bow line rope to Mr. Leek so he could assist in tying the boat to the dock. Joe did not smile much. He wanted to always show strength with no dent in his manly armor. Some big men who are really not a threat pretend to be something they are not. They seem to bluff their way through life because of their size and fake attitude. Big Joe Croom was just such a man. He had a coward's mind with a hero's body. After he tied off the bow line, he threw the stern line to Mr. Leek.

"We had a good night, Al. Hell, we caught about eight boxes. Probably should have stayed out for a few more drags, but I just didn't want to. Sometimes ya just gotta go with your gut, ya know? I had a feelin' I needed to be home."

Mr. Leek did not want to be the messenger. "That gut feelin' we get can be pretty strong sometimes." Mr. Leek stepped off of the dock and onto the deck of the boat. He had Big Joe's full attention. "It's Stella, Joe. There's been some kinda accident."

Joe's face went white and his stomach burned. "What do you mean a accident?"

Pee Wee found her on the front porch this morning. The police are at your house right now. I'm sorry, Joe; she's gone."

Mr. King walked out onto his front porch with his first cup of coffee. He had slept later than usual, due to the fact he struggled with his dreams during the night. He did not want to fall back to sleep in fear of continuing the dream with Anna Jo and the drifter. The possibility that Anna Jo had the power to walk in his dreams made him uneasy. It was different if he used the carousel to bring her to him for sex, but he did not want her being in control of what went on in his mind when he slept.

Mary C. lay in her bed snuggled up to Billy. He was the best bed partner a grandmother could have. She did think about Jack Jarvis for a moment, but he was in the past.

Sofia was at the store for another morning shift, hoping to see Jason sometime during the day. Surely, he would be looking for her after their wonderful night together. As she thought about how she wanted him, Jason was kneeling behind Theda Moore while she screamed and pushed her butt cheeks back toward him as hard as she could. As Theda's voice bounded off the bedroom wall, Jason wished Rebecca Coolie was there with them to kiss Theda for him.

Big Joe Croom stopped his truck a few yards away from his front yard. There were three police cars and an ambulance blocking his way. He was sick to his stomach when he saw a blood soaked white sheet covering something near the porch. He knew it was Stella. Officer Boos moved away from the sheet and walk to Big Joe. "Mr. Croom, I'm David Boos, sir. It's your wife."

Big Joe looked at the sheet, but nodded his head and talked to the officer. "Mr. Leek told me." He walked toward Stella's body. "What happened?"

"One of your boys found her out here early this morning. Looks like she's been out here all night. And we don't know what happened."

Big Joe stood next to the sheet. "Mr. Leek said it was some kinda accident."

Officer Paul Short walked up. "It could be an accident, maybe a fall, but we think somebody killed her. Did your wife wear any jewelry, sir?"

"Her wedding ring. A watch sometimes, but not at night. I just gave her a new ruby heart necklace yesterday. Can I see her?"

Officer Boos took a deep breath. "Of course, sir, but we just don't think it's a good idea. We can't stop you, but it's not a good thing under these conditions."

Big Joe knelt down on the ground next to Stella's body, reached out a trembling hand and lifted up the bloody sheet. The material stuck to her hair as he pulled the sheet up. It looked almost like she moved. It took Joe's heart for a second. When he saw her swollen and distorted head, he dropped the sheet back down. Joe Croom stepped away from his dead wife.

"You were right. I shouldn't have done that. Where are my boys?"

Paul Short had the answer. "We had an officer take them to your sister's house. We thought that would be what you wanted."

"Yes, thanks. Were they okay?"

"The little one found her; he was quiet and didn't talk to us. One of the medics went over there to be sure he wasn't in shock. The other two boys were quiet, too, but they moved away from us and sat together under that tree." Officer Short pointed at a large fig tree on the side of the yard.

"I'd better get over there and be with the boys. First Joe, and now this. What's it gonna do to 'em?"

"They've got a strong father; they'll bounce back and be fine."

Big Joe nodded at the compliment and went to his truck. He looked back at the sheet. "Where will you take her?"

Paul Short still had the answer. "She'll have to go to the coroner's office first. We'll let you know what's next as soon as we can. We'll take care of her, sir. Just go take care of your boys."

The bloody face of the drifter flashed in Big Joe's face. He got out of the truck and walked to Officer Boos. "There was a man yesterday looking for a handout. I got mad at his poor manners and comments to Stella. I beat him up pretty bad and left him at the sand hill. He done come back lookin' for me and killed Stella."

The drifter had not left Mayport as Mary C. had mandated. He was standing at the ferry slip looking toward the other side of the St. Johns River. He turned to see two police cars driving up next to him. Four policemen with pistols drawn approached him. He held up his hand as he did with Mary C.

"Just gettin' ready to catch the next ferry, fellas. Y'all sure want my skinny ass gone, don't ya? You don't have to point them guns at me; I'm really goin' this time."

Paul Short took the lead. "Put your hands on your head mister, or you die right here."

The man put his hands on his head as directed. "Y'all really kill folks for just walkin' around in your town? This is a bad ass little place."

Two of the officers approached the drifter and forced him to the ground. He did not struggle, so it was easy to handcuff him. They stood him up and went through his pockets. One officer checking his pockets pulled out the ten dollar bill Mary C. had given him. He then pulled out Stella Croom's wedding ring Mary C. had also dropped into his pocket when she stuffed in the ten. The officer pulled out Stella's new heart-shaped ruby necklace. Paul Short took the items from the other officer. He looked at David Boos and then turned and slammed the drifter to the ground. "You're under arrest for the murder of Stella Croom, you sack of shit." He pointed his pistol at the drifter's head. "Please run so I can save the tax payers the money it costs to hang your sorry ass."

Jack Jarvis' body was transported to his home town of West Ocean City, Maryland. Before he was buried in the family plot, there was a big party with friends and relatives at the Stummbin' Inn Bar, one of his favorite watering holes when he was home.

Mary C. did not attend the services, because it was on the same day as Fabian's funeral, and it was too far away. Besides, she had only known Jack Jarvis for a little less than two days. She would not attend Stella's funeral either.

On the day of Stella's funeral, Mary C. did go to Stella's house and take her blue Ford Falcon back. She saw it the night she killed Stella. It was on the side of the house with grass growing up around the tires. Mary C. hated the thought that Betsy was just sitting there and not rolling on the road. She figured Big Joe would know she took it, and if he didn't she still didn't care. Mary C. gave the car to young Joe, not Stella nor Big Joe.

After Fabian's funeral, Theda's uncle arrived at Theda's house with a police escort and took her and her baby back to Fort Myers with him and his wife. He had gotten a court order to become the legal guardian of the fifteen-year-old mother and her baby. They had decided that Theda was too young to raise the child alone. Theda was fond of her uncle and knew he was truly interested in helping her, but she did not want to leave Jason and her house. A *For Sale* sign went up in Theda's front yard.

If you had the money, it did not take very long to build a Jim Walter Home. Mary C. had the money. She had already selected her Deluxe Model to be built on five acres of land she bought next to Miss Carolyn's house out on Mayport Road. Mary C. had also paid for a deluxe treatment for Miss Carolyn's Jim Walter Home that was built six months before.

Mary C. drove her blue Ford Falcon off the main road and stopped in the knee high grass and weeds of her new property. Sofia was sitting in the passenger's seat holding Billy in her lap. Mary C. stepped out of the car and stood in the tall grass. As she slowly turned her head admiring her new possession, the sound of a familiar voice brought a smile to her face.

"Yoo-hoo, yoo-hoo." Mary C. turned to see Miss Carolyn walking thought the high weeds, coming in her direction. Mary C. continued to smile as she watched Miss Carolyn lift her legs up high to get through the grass. Miss Carolyn managed to make it to where Mary C. was standing. She threw her arms around Mary C.'s neck. "God bless you, darlin', but you didn't have to do such a wonderful thing."

Mary C. knew Miss Carolyn was referring to her generous gift of the Jim Walter Deluxe treatment. "You deserve it, Miss Carolyn. I'm happy to do it. Now, let's not talk about it anymore. What do you think of my five acres?"

Miss Carolyn was all smiles. "Darlin', it's a beautiful piece of land. I'm so pleased and excited about you being my neighbor. I hear they're gonna start clearin' and buildin' next week."

Mary C. loved Miss Carolyn's kind and sincere nature. "That's what they tell me. They say I can move in two months, but we'll see."

Miss Carolyn changed the subject when she noticed Sofia sitting in the car. "Hey, darlin', I didn't see ya there. I was just carryin' on and lost my manners."

Sofia smiled. "That's okay, Miss Carolyn; we're all excited about Mary C.'s new house."

Miss Carolyn saw Billy. "Look at this baby. What beautiful skin and features. What a true Honey Child. He looks like a little Indian baby, don't he?"

Sofia looked down at Billy. Mary C. smiled. "He really does look like an Indian, Miss Carolyn."

Miss Carolyn moved to the side of the car. "Do you think he'll let me hold him?"

Sofia's ice-blue eyes opened wide as she smiled one of her usually perfect, straight, white teeth smile. "Yes, ma'am. He'll go to anybody."

Mary C. chimed in. "He has no fear."

Miss Carolyn looked back at Mary C. as she lifted Billy up into her arms. "A golden honey child with no fear. I've heard folks call him an oak baby." Sofia's eyes flashed as Miss Carolyn maneuvered him into her arms. Sofia wanted to tell what she knew. "You're right, he's golden, and his father is, too. The Indian priest told me that before he died."

Mary C. had to join in. "Now, don't start all that oak baby talk, you two. I don't think I can take it."

Miss Carolyn looked into Billy's big eyes. "Well, you know as a Catholic, I don't believe in no magic oak tree, but anyone can see this baby is special. It don't take magic to see that. You can see it in his big beautiful eyes. Look at the size of his eyes."

Mary C. had to tell what she knew. "He's got his mama's eyes. Right out of her head. He's got Jessie's eyes." Sofia looked down and did not talk. She did not like hearing about Jessie.

Miss Carolyn did not know the meaning behind Mary C.'s odd comment about Billy's eyes. She had her own thoughts. "This child is special like my Little George. He's as golden as they come. He's my Honey Child."

Mary C. could not resist. "Now, Miss Carolyn, you gonna have me and Sofia thinkin' you did the deed under the oak tree. Your Little George ain't no oak baby, is he?"

Sofia's eyes flashed again. Miss Carolyn was surprised at the question. "Heavens no! I think I would have remembered bein' at the tree. He's just got somethin' special; it ain't got nothin' to do with that tree." Miss Carolyn changed the subject and looked at Mary C. "Where's that handsome son of yours anyway?"

Mary C. welcomed the new topic. "Jason's gettin' the boat ready for shrimpin' again."

Miss Carolyn smiled and kissed Billy on his cheek. "As handsome as that boy is, he'll probably bring a mermaid back to the dock." She smiled at her own little joke. "I could just eat this little Honey Child up."

Sofia did not like the mermaid comment. She had decided to find her feelings for Jason and hated the fact there were always other women in his life, even a mythical creature like a mermaid.

The noise of a truck engine caused the three ladies to turn in the direction of Miss Carolyn's house. A big closed truck with Jim Walter written on the side was rolling into Miss Carolyn's front yard. She turned to Mary C. "Come on y'all, let's see if Jim Walter himself has come a callin'."

Mary C., Miss Carolyn and Sofia sat at Miss Carolyn's kitchen table. Billy was asleep on the couch with pillows around him. The Jim Walter workers were bringing in the material needed for the deluxe treatment. Miss Carolyn joked with one of the workers. "Jim didn't come with y'all?"

The worker smiled. "No, ma'am. I don't think I've ever seen him. Is he a real person?" He looked at Mary C. and Sofia. "How you ladies doin'?"

Sofia took his heart with her smile. "We're just fine. We're excited about what you're doing." The sound of a car horn ended the worker's moment with the beautiful young Sofia.

Miss Carolyn looked out her kitchen window. "It's somebody in a pretty red truck. Speakin' of the devil. I think it's that handsome boy of yours, Mary C." Sofia moved to the window as the worker went about his business. Mary C. smiled at his obvious disappointment.

Sofia was excited to see Jason. She liked feeling that way again. It was natural, and she was trying to forget how awful she was after their life-changing adventure while on their way to the Giant's Motel. She watched Jason walk toward the house. "I think he's bought a new red truck, Miss Mary C."

Mary C. smiled at Sofia's beaming face. She was glad the young beauty was finding herself again. Jason walked through the opened door. Miss Carolyn was funny. "There's a handsome young man in my house. Hey, darlin'." She looked at Mary C. "Ain't that a Conway Twitty song?"

Mary C. actually laughed out loud. "I think it's 'Hello, darlin', not 'hey, darlin'."

"Yeah, that's it." She looked at Jason again and greeted him in her best low Conway Twitty voice. "Hello Darlin'." Miss Carolyn hugged Jason's neck. "That's some truck you've got out there."

Mary C. loved Miss Carolyn. "Let's go see it." The foursome walked into the front yard to see the new truck. Miss Carolyn stood back, so the others could be together. She always thought about others. It was her way.

Mary C. turned back to be sure Miss Carolyn was with them. "I can't stand it nomore, here." Mary C. handed Miss Carolyn the keys to the new red truck. "The truck's yours. Jason was just the delivery boy."

Miss Carolyn was in a daze. "Dear God, a red truck for me. Lord have mercy on my soul."

Mary C. knew what it meant to Miss Carolyn. "Red's the only color for women like me and you. Course, I ain't had too much luck with red cars lately, but it's still my favorite."

"Ain't that the Gospel truth. Red's our color, alright." She turned and hugged Mary C. "I don't know what to say, darlin'. This is too much for my little brain to handle. Are you sure you can do this?"

"It's done."

Miss Carolyn had an idea. "Let's take her down Seminole Road and drive on the beach to Bill's Hideaway."

Mary C. turned to Jason. "You take Sofia home in my car. Miss Carolyn will take me home when we're finished. I'll be there when I get there."

Sofia was excited to be with Jason and Billy. It was like they were married and had a baby. John King sat on his bed looking at the music box carousel. Anna Jo Hamilton was on his mind. He wanted her to come to him.

Officer Boos stood with Paul Short staring into an empty jail cell. "He can't just be gone. Someone had to let him out." He turned to Paul Short. "Let's get out to Mayport in case this nut ball goes back to the scene of the crime."

Miss Carolyn turned off of the wooden ramp and onto the sand at Seminole Beach. She and Mary C. could see Bill's Hideaway ahead of them next to the Big Jetties. The new truck did not kick up any sand as Miss Carolyn drove at a proper speed. There was a woman walking on the beach near the water. She wore a long black dress. Mary C. looked out the passenger's side window and thought the woman looked like Zulmary. "Stop, Miss Carolyn. You know this lady?"

Miss Carolyn looked out the front window. "I don't think so."

The woman turned to the truck and walk toward them. Mary C.'s eyes widened as the woman came closer. Mary C. realized it was Anna Jo. She felt her heart skip an irregular beat. Anna Jo was standing next to the window. Her voice was like something in the distant wind. "Hello, Mary C." Anna Jo looked at Miss Carolyn. "Hello, Miss Carolyn."

Miss Carolyn knew Anna Jo Hamilton considered herself a witch. She had no words. Mary C. responded.

"When I heard you were out at Black Hammock, I knew you'd come here next."

"I'm here to save you and Mayport. It's my destiny."

Miss Carolyn found her voice. "Would you like a ride, darlin',or did ya bring your broom?"

Mary C. shook her head and smiled. Miss Carolyn was too much. Anna Jo smiled a half smile and answered. "No thank you, Miss Carolyn. I need to be one with the elements if I'm going to fulfill my destiny."

"You use that word a lot, don't ya? I don't know too many folks who say 'destiny' that much. You just need some good old blessed rosary beads."

"I'll pass on the Catholic rituals, Miss Carolyn, but thank you for your kind thought." She looked deep into Mary C.'s eyes. "I'll have to get stronger if I am to win this battle. You will supply the strength I need. You've always been the strongest. You may even have to lead the way." Mary C. ignored Anna Jo's comments.

Miss Carolyn was the kindest individual you could ever meet, but she had heard enough from the dramatic witch. "Well, I'm leadin' the way to Bill's. Are ya sure you wouldn't like a ride with us? I hate to disappoint ya, but I don't think he cooks children any more, but I'm sure the mullet dip is still on the tables."

Anna Jo continued her stare with Mary C. and did not care about Miss Carolyn's sarcasm. "You two go on ahead. I think he's waiting for me, and I'm not ready. The ocean water and the sand will make me stronger. I should be fine by the time I get there."

Miss Carolyn smiled. "Okay then, nice seein' ya." She stepped on the gas pedal, spinning the new truck tires in the soft sand of Seminole Beach. Mary C. looked into the side view mirror as the truck moved away. She saw Anna Jo continue her walk.

Miss Carolyn drove her new truck right up under Bill's Hideaway between the pylons that held the building up off of the beach sand. They both got out and walked to the outside stairs leading to the main restaurant above. Mary C. could see Anna Jo about a half a mile down the beach still walking toward them. She glanced at the big jetty rocks as a group of children chased some Florida blue crabs under the red rocks. A man stood on the rocks. Mary C. took a few steps toward the rocks to get a better look at him. Her heart skipped a beat when she focused her eyes on the drifter. He was not looking at Mary C. He was looking down the beach at Anna Jo. Mary C. had no idea he was standing on Jason's lunch rock. Anna Jo Hamilton was the only one who knew a Ditch Walker had arrived in Mayport.